Sassy's Place

A Darcy Jean Mystery, Ep. 1

TERRY JOE GUNNELS

Inquiries and Book Orders should be addressed to:

Gunnels Publishing
Email: terrygunnels51@cox.net
Phone: 757-930-1596

ISBN: 979-8-89175-208-5 (hc)
ISBN: 979-8-89175-198-9 (sc)
ISBN: 979-8-89175-199-6 (e)

CONTENTS

ACKNOWLEDGMENTS

To my wife, Shirley Jean (Cookie), for encouraging me through almost five decades of marriage in all projects I have undertaken. And for spending untold hours proofreading every one of my manuscripts for errors.

To my editor, Donje Putnam, whom I have known since she was a teenager and my daughter's best friend. She always nails me to the wall with corrections and suggestions. I thank her.

1. To Dianne Ahl who did a great job beta reading, and found so many of my mistakes, and made great suggestions for re-writes.
2. To Sterling Norris Monk, and his lovely wife, Bruce Monk, for reading, giving feedback, and finding errors I missed.
3. To Donald Emond, a lifelong friend who gave me some insightful comments.
4. To Donna Brennan, who read the manuscript and added some interesting comments.
5. To Debby Groome Wilkerson, who gave me valuable feedback and constructive thoughts.
6. To Pamela Double, my realtor, and property manager who gave me some great suggestions.

Special thanks to Ellie Summers, of **E-Summers Creative Solutions**, who has helped me publish every one of my books. She has guided me and made sure that the ghost publisher made my printed books the absolute best and highest quality they can be.

To all others, for exciting me to move forward with the story and encouraging me to publish,

I give my heartfelt THANK YOU to every person involved with this book.

CHAPTER ONE

Sassafras Magill, or Sassy as she was called by her friends, woke up and grabbed the pole she used to help her get in and out of bed each day. She had cerebral palsy. Her arms and legs sometimes just went where they wanted instead of where she wanted them to be. That was okay. She had learned to deal with her disability. She got up, dressed, and headed to the bathroom to brush her teeth and comb her hair. Most mornings she woke up with the muscles in her arms and legs stiff. She always did basic stretching exercises to loosen her muscles. After that, she slogged her way down the stairs of her apartment, which was located above the store. It was also something she had learned to do. Her entire body just ached some days, but she knew it was part of her condition. It was going to be a beautiful day for her. She was going to make it a good day. After turning the gas pumps on from a panel inside the store area, she unlocked the front door.

Sassy ran the small convenience store and gas station after her parents retired. That was ten years ago. She tried to get to see her parents about once a week, but she spent a lot of time at the store.

She saw Josh sitting on a bench outside. Beside him was a hand truck loaded with some items she had ordered to restock the store.

"Good morning, Sassy. How are you today?" he asked.

"Hello, Josh. I'm fine. You're here early. Don't you have other deliveries to make?"

"Yep, sure do, but you don't have a large order, so I can unload it and still be done by the end of the day. It will only take a few minutes, and I'll be on my way."

"Thank you so much, Josh. You're always so kind."

Josh was a delivery person for the company she purchased her food items from for her little store. He would bring her order and help her by assisting with stocking the shelves. Helping her was not part of his job, but he always took time to do it.

As a car pulled up to the pumps, an old fashion bell rang inside the store. The bell let her know customers were there in case they needed to come inside and pick up a few things.

She looked out the storefront windows and saw one of her favorite customers. He pumped his gas and came inside to pay. Her parents had upgraded the pumps many years before to accept credit cards and allowed customers to pay at the pump. This customer always came inside to pay.

"Good morning, Sassy. How are you doing today?" he said as he pulled out his credit card and waited for her to come to the register.

She smiled back at him. "Good morning to you, Mickey Ray. I keep telling you, it's much faster to pay at the pump."

"And I keep telling you, I enjoy seeing your smiling face. Are Jaime and Reilly here yet? I was hoping for a hot cup of coffee."

"Not yet. They'll be here in a few minutes. I always let them come in half an hour after I open. It lets me get things set up for the day. I let Jaime make the coffee. She enjoys doing that. It's hard for me to handle the coffee carafe," she said as she took his credit card with her gnarled fingers to make the sale.

Mickey Ray Christianson was a real estate developer. He had taken over his father's business a few years ago when his father was injured and his mother killed in a car accident. He owned many apartments in Bridgeton, including the one where Sassy's parents lived, and ran the biggest construction company in the state. Bridgeton was a small-town midway between Williamsburg and Richmond, Virginia. He met Sassy, and they bonded as friends when she took over the store.

Just then, the door opened and in came Jaime. She also smiled and spoke to him. "Hi, Mr. Christianson."

"Good morning, Jaime. How are you today?"

"I'm fine. I'm always fine when you are here," she said.

"Every time I see you, you make my day a little better," Mickey added with a smile.

She blushed and walked to a shelf and moved a couple of canned goods back in their correct places. "I wish people wouldn't move things out of place," she said to no one in particular.

"Would you make a pot of coffee for Mr. Christianson, please, Jaime?" asked Sassy.

Jaime had Down syndrome. She was a soft-spoken, sweet-natured person who helped Sassy stock shelves and keep the store in order. She could ring up basic cash sales at the register. If she had trouble or got confused, she would ask Reilly for help.

Reilly was Sassy's other helper. He was a high-functioning autistic young man. His strength was in math, and he could use the register and ring up sales. He had an uncanny ability to add up the sales and compute the sales tax in his head faster than it could be put into the register. Sassy always insisted that he use the register so customers could get a receipt. He was so fast that customers would throw in a few extra items just to see him calculate the total in his head. Sassy noticed that her sales went up after she hired Reilly.

She understood the feelings and attitudes of other physically disabled people because she was handicapped. With that in mind, she wanted to hire people with disabilities.

Mostly, people were kind and considerate of Sassy and her workers, but there were always a few people who were rude. Sometimes their rudeness hurt, but she tried to make each day a winning day for herself and her co-workers.

"Don't want to put you or Jaime out this early, Sassy," said Mickey.

"You are never putting us out. We are inconveniencing you by not having fresh hot coffee when we open," Sassy said, wiping off the counter by the register. "If you have time, have a seat in the chair over there by the table in the corner. We'll bring it to you. It's on the house since you have to wait for it," she added. Mickey always overlooked her slurred speech, which was caused by her cerebral palsy. She was sweet, and he liked her.

Sometimes when Mickey had time, he would sit and talk with Sassy and her workers. They were nice, and he enjoyed their company. Reilly talked little, and Mickey knew that many autistic people did not connect well with people and shied away from conversation.

Today he wasn't busy or in a rush, so he sat. He watched Jaime make the coffee. Sassy came over and sat in the other chair at the table.

"So, Mickey, how's business?" she drawled. Even through her slurred speech, she had a Southern accent.

"It's going well. Things are a bit slow now. I'm always glad of a break. For me, a slow day is a good day," he said. "How are things with Kevin?"

"Fine. He still has a few more days, and he'll graduate law school."

"That sounds great. Will he go into private practice or join a local firm?" Mickey asked.

"I don't know. He'll probably go to work with another firm until we save enough money to start a practice of his own. He'll have to rent an office and hire someone as a secretary. It will take some money to get started. We just don't have that kind of money right now."

"Thank you, Jamie," he said with a smile when Jaime set a cup of coffee on the table, and put some creamer and sugar out for him. "But I'm sure it won't be long until he has his own practice. Maybe we can even throw some business his way."

"That would be nice. We would really appreciate it," she said.

"Well, I guess I'd better get to the office. I have a lot of paperwork to get done." He called to Jaime, "Thank you for the coffee. You make the best coffee in town." He looked at Sassy. "See you in a few days," he said as he walked out the door.

"He's always so nice," said Jaime.

Reilly had come in while Mickey was there and helped Jamie. A few minutes later, the door buzzer rang, and they all looked to see who had come in. It was Kevin Samson, Sassy's boyfriend. They had been dating for over two years, and she was helping him with living expenses and his tuition in law school.

Ignoring Jaime and Reilly, he called out loudly, "Hello, Sassy!" as he headed for the back room where Sassy was taking inventory.

"Hi, Kevin!" she answered, and leaned to give him a quick kiss.

"I can't stay long. I just thought I would stop by on my way back to the apartment. I need to study for my final exams."

"Will you be a lawyer then?"

"No, I still have to pass the BAR exam to actually be a lawyer. It'll still take me a few months to take those."

She took a deep breath. "This's taking so long. I just want it to be done."

He took her hand and pulled her close. "I know, but we are now coming to an end. I'll take the BAR exam in a couple of months, and then we'll be free!"

"Free? What do you mean, free?" she said.

"You know. Free from all the stress of school, exams and waiting for all this to end."

"Um, okay. I guess so."

"Hey, the car needs an oil change. Do you have a few dollars so I can get it done? It's your car, and I want to take care of it, so it will last us for a long time," he stated.

"My purse is upstairs. I'll go get it."

"Don't worry, it's easier if I get it. I know how hard it is for you to climb the stairs. One day, we'll get you one of those chair lifts to help you get up and down the stairs," he said as he moved toward the stairs.

"Sure, we'll have more money when we don't have your college tuition. We'll get married, and you can move in here instead of renting an apartment. My purse is on my dresser in the bedroom," she called to him as he went upstairs.

He found her purse and took most of her cash but still left her a few dollars to spend.

He came back down a couple of minutes later. "I took what I needed for the oil change, and some more to buy gas. I hope you don't mind." He gave her a quick kiss on the cheek and left.

Each day passed slowly. She was looking forward to Kevin finishing his exams and taking the BAR exam. It took almost all her free money to help him, but she knew it would be worth it when he finished.

Things were going fine at the store. Reilly and Jaime we so much comfort just to be around. The two people who were always checking on her were Josh and her friend, Charles Duncan, a cab driver. Josh had only been in town a few months and had moved her delivery time to the afternoon. When he had time, he would sit and talk with her just like Charles. Charles stopped by to fill up his cab about once a week, sometimes more if he had a busy week. Charles owned his own cab, and they had become friends when they were both in high school together many years ago. He was even-tempered until someone laughed or made fun of her or her disability. He was like a big brother to her, giving her deep discounts on her fares when she called him for rides. She didn't have enough money to buy her own car because she had bought Kevin a car to drive to and from school.

Kevin called her almost daily to tell her about his progress and how things were going. His last call was several days ago, and he told her he wouldn't be available for the following week because he had so many things to take care of. He finally called her and said he had some special news to give her, so he had made reservations at Luigi's for Friday night.

"That sounds great, Kevin. I've missed you so much. Can't you give me a hint about the news?"

"Sorry. No can do!" he exclaimed. "All I can say is, it will end all your emotional and financial troubles. You will be much happier when I tell you. I can't say anymore until I get the final answer in a few days."

Her mind reeled with the dreams of his news. She imagined it was the culmination of all her dreams for the past two years. She knew what his news was going to be. He was going to officially propose to her.

She was happy. The next few days passed slowly, but she didn't mind. Josh came in near the end of the day with her latest stock order.

"Hello, Sassy. Wow, you are gleaming today," he said with a smile. Josh was a handsome man she had met several months ago when he started driving the delivery truck to her store. He was tall and so handsome.

"Yes. I have wonderful news. I've been on top of the world," she answered.

"Can you tell me about it?" he said as he stopped and set the hand-truck that was loaded with store stock. He brushed back his dark wavy hair to get it out of his face.

She looked toward Jaime and Reilly and motioned him to the back stockroom. "I don't want to tell them yet. As wonderful as they are, they might say something without meaning to. You know what I mean?" she whispered.

He leaned against a stack of boxes. "I understand." He reached up and made a motion of zipping up his lips, and looked down at her with his dreamy dark eyes.

"I think Kevin's going to propose to me at dinner Friday night," she gushed.

He reached out and gave her a huge hug. "I'm so glad for you, Sassy." When he pulled back, a tear was running down his face. She noticed the smile was still on his face, but it lacked the usual spark of happiness she always noticed.

"It's what we've been working toward almost since we met. I can't wait until it's official."

"You're my favorite customer. You've really made my day!" he said seriously. "It's getting a bit late, so let's get this stock put away, and I have to get back to the warehouse."

Jamie, Reilly and Josh put the stock on the shelves, and Josh left. Jaime looked at Sassy and asked, "What was wrong with Josh?"

"What do you mean, Jaime?"

"He was happy when he came in, but sad when he left. Why?"

"It's all in your imagination. He was fine," Sassy answered.

"Okay, if you say so, but he seemed sad to me," Jaime said as she went back to work.

Later that day, Charles stopped by to fill up his cab. When he came in, Sassy was waiting for him at the back, and she motioned for him to come back to the stockroom.

"Where have you been, Charles? I've been waiting for you all week," she said excitedly.

"Well, um, I had a fare that went to the Newport News Airport, and I had to fill up there. Then another one all the way on the other side of town and..."

"Never mind that, I know you have to fill up and it can't always be here," she said.

Charles interrupted her with, "I always try to fill up here."

She waved her hand at him to hush. "I know. I know. Just listen to me for a minute."

"Okay. What are you so excited about, Sassy?"

"I have wonderful news. You're my best friend in the world, and I've been waiting to tell you."

"Why didn't you call me?" he asked.

"I wanted to tell you face to face. I wanted to see your expression when I told you, silly!"

"What? Tell me. I'm here now. Stop fussing at me and tell me," he said, now getting excited for her.

"Kevin's going to propose to me on Friday!" she gushed.

He threw up his hands, grabbed her and swung her around, then set her down gently. "Tell me all about it. That's wonderful news, Sassy!"

"I know. Isn't it great? I have to get a new dress for the occasion. I have to call my mother, and we can go shopping for a new dress."

"Yes, it may be odd, but I want to be your chauffeur for that shopping trip. I'll take you and your mother to every dress shop in town, if you will let me. You are like my girlfriend, except in a sisterly way, I mean."

"I know. I know what you mean. It will be the three of us. But I have to pay you."

"No. I will not allow you to do that. It'll be part of my wedding present to you. I'll rent a limousine and drive you to the wedding. It'll be so much fun for me."

"Okay, but now you must go to work. I know that will cost you a lot, so you need to work. Get out of here, Charles," she said, pushing him out the doorway.

He got to his car and blew her a kiss. She acted as if she had caught it and placed her hand on her cheek. She waved goodbye to him as he drove off.

The rest of the week went by uneventfully, and on Friday morning, Mickey Christianson walked into the store again to pay for his gas.

"Good morning, ladies, and you too, Reilly," he said as he handed Reilly his credit card. "How is everyone doing?"

Reilly just silently ran the credit card and rang up the sale. Jamie smiled and answered Mickey with a smile, "I'm fine."

"And you, Sassy. How are things going for you and Kevin?"

"They're going fine. He passed the BAR exam a few weeks ago and is looking for a job now. I hope he finds one soon. He hasn't worked for such a long time. He wanted to concentrate on his law studies, so I've been helping him out financially."

"You have been supporting him all this time?" Mickey asked.

"Yes. We planned on getting married when he finished college, passed the BAR and got a job. This place provides me with a decent living, but it gets pretty tight when I'm supporting myself, and him too."

"I understand," Mickey said sadly. "He could have worked at least part-time so as not to put such a strain on you."

"I guess he could have, but I love him, and he loves me. I'll do anything I can to help him be successful. We want so much out of life. Few men would want someone like me."

"You are different, but not in a bad way. He's the lucky one. Not you."

"I hope you're right. We are having dinner today. He said he had some news for me. He is going to make an official proposal. I just know he is, Mickey."

"I bet he will, and when you say, YES, I will gift you a full honeymoon trip!"

"Oh, Mickey, that is so sweet, but you don't have to do that!" she exclaimed.

Mickey furrowed his brow. "I know I don't have to do it. I want to do it. You're doing a great service here. You're helping other people by giving them jobs, and you've been so giving by paying Kevin's expenses. It's the least I can do."

She reached over to take Mickey's hand in hers. "God bless you, Mickey Ray Christianson. You are a true godsend."

Mickey got up, leaned over to her and kissed her on the forehead. "It's my blessing to know you, Sassafras Magill."

She looked up at him and said with a huge grin on her face, "We won't be friends much longer if you call me Sassafras again!"

He grinned at her. "I have to go, but you call me when he proposes, and I'll tell my sister Darcy Jean to plan your dream wedding and honeymoon. I would do it myself, but I'm a guy. What do I know about planning a wedding? Women just know how to do those things," he said, rolling his eyes as he walked out the door, and waved goodbye to Jaime.

CHAPTER TWO

s the day went on, approaching closing time, customers came
and went. Some came in to buy small convenience items like
a loaf of bread or milk. Sassy didn't approve of smoking or
drinking alcohol, but they both had good mark-ups, so she stocked
them for sale in the store.

She went back upstairs to her apartment above the store and
showered to get ready for her dinner with Kevin. He had told her to
meet him at Luigi's for dinner. Luigi's was the nicest restaurant in
Bridgeton. She was so excited and wanted to look especially nice when
Kevin proposed to her. She knew she had a pretty face. Her body shape
was good for her condition, but she wanted to feel special for this
momentous occasion, so she bought a new dress when Charles took her
and her mother shopping. Charles said she looked very alluring when
he saw her in it. Most of the time, she didn't care that her limbs were
twisted and sometimes she couldn't control them. Kevin had always
been very attentive, making her feel special. She was what was called
a spastic quadriplegic, which meant that her cerebral palsy affected
all four limbs and her speech. She could walk and function normally,
with a few exceptions. Her gnarled hands caused some difficulty with
tasks requiring manual dexterity. She could one-finger type slowly, and
even work the register in the store, but it was extremely hard for her to
button her clothes. She tried to buy clothes with zippers instead. Even
zippers with tiny flaps were a challenge to pull up. Velcro was almost a
necessity for things like her shoes.

She had felt so bad about herself for so long. Then she met Kevin. He had treated her special. They made plans together. He used to work at a local law office as a research staff member. When he applied to William and Mary Law School in Williamsburg, he continued at the law firm. The law firm had him working long hours in research, and Kevin didn't have the time to devote himself to his studies. He tried to help Sassy with her store. Even working part-time hours, he told her he couldn't study and work, so he quit and she hired Reilly to help with the books. She agreed to support Kevin financially until he finished school. They didn't live together, so Kevin had his own apartment.

Now, it would all come home. They would get married. He would give up his apartment and move in with her above the store. Yes, it might be lean for a while, but when he got a job as an attorney, things would get better. Maybe someday they would have children. She was very happy. Things were wonderful. Finally, all her dreams were about to come true.

She finished putting on a little makeup and went downstairs before she called for a taxi to take her to the restaurant. "What do you think, guys?" she said to Jaime and Reilly.

Jaime looked up with her beautiful, innocent grin. She cocked her head aside like a dog does when it is assessing a situation. "You look so pretty, Sassy. I love your dress."

"Thank you, Jaime. What do you think, Reilly?" she asked.

Reilly looked at her with a blank look on his face. "You look fine."

It was a suitable answer for Reilly. He didn't say much, and she understood how he was.

"Thank you, Reilly. Can the two of you manage the store while I'm gone? I should be back in a couple of hours. If I'm not back by closing time, just turn out the lights and lock the door behind you. I'll take care of the rest when I get home tonight." They were both intellectually disabled, but could still do simple jobs in the store. If something came up, she always carried her cell phone with her. She had allowed them to lock the store in the past, and she knew they could do it tonight if she was late.

When the taxi arrived, Charles got out and opened the door for her and helped her inside. He was also dressed up for the occasion. He looked at her and grinned. "Wow. You look amazing, girl. Even prettier than you looked in the dress shop when we picked it out!"

"Thank you, Charles. You and mother did a wonderful job of helping me pick out the perfect dress. I love Daddy, but he was so glad he didn't have to go with us. He hates any kind of shopping for clothes. Even when the clothes are for him. Anyway, you look quite handsome yourself."

"Thanks, I wanted to look nice to take my special friend to this very special occasion tonight. I hope he sweeps you off your feet! Okay, we're off to see the wizard!" he said as he stepped on the gas and pulled into traffic.

When they arrived, he came around and helped her out of the car. "I wish you a lifetime of happiness, Sas. You know I have loved you like a sister ever since we were in high school together."

"I know you do, and I love you like a brother too. Since I probably won't be riding back home with you, I'll settle up with you now." She handed him several bills, including a generous tip.

"I told you. This one's on me!" he said as he gently pushed her hands away.

"Tonight is going to be special for me, so I want to share my joy with you."

"You're the sweetest girl in the world, Sassy. Now, go get your proposal," he laughed.

Kevin was already here and seated, so she proceeded to his table and sat down. She leaned over and kissed him as she sat down. Kevin motioned to the server and ordered the best champagne they had.

He asked her how her day was going so far.

"It's going wonderfully so far. I'm so excited to be here with you," she said with her eyes glowing with excitement. "We haven't been here in such a long time."

"You look so pretty tonight. It that a new dress?"

"Yes. I got it just for this occasion," she answered.

"We've both been so busy. Me with my studies and you with the store. We haven't talked in several days," he said.

"I know, and I've missed you so much. I was so excited for you when you called last night and told me you already had a job offer. Why didn't you call me sooner?"

"Let's order first and enjoy our dinner. Then we'll talk," he suggested.

They ordered and talked about business and the store. She told him that when they had children, they could add to the back of the store for a nursery during the day. She could still continue working at the store while he went to work each day. As they talked, the food came, and as they ate, Kevin began talking.

"That's what I wanted to talk to you about."

"Okay," she smiled and looked at him. She loved this man so much. She thought he was very handsome. His thick blonde hair and crystal blue eyes. What did she ever do to deserve a man like him?

Yes, she was pretty in the face, but it was a genuine effort just to keep her long brown hair combed throughout the day. She didn't wear makeup like most women, because much of the work in the store was not conducive to wearing makeup. She was constantly washing her hands, and when the stock came in, she did what she could to help unpack the boxes. Though Reilly helped with heavy items, she always ended the day looking disheveled. Even her clothes were not fashionable, but utilitarian.

Kevin always dressed as if to enter a GQ contest. With all he had, he was hers.

He looked down at the plate sitting in front of him and back up at her. "What's the matter?" she asked.

He just shook his head. "I got the letter telling me I had passed the BAR a month ago."

"That's good, but why didn't you tell me then? Why did you wait so long to tell me?"

"Because I was putting in applications for a job."

"I get that. So, you wanted to tell me all this at one time, so we could have one big celebration. Right?" she said, leaning over the table to get closer to him.

"Yes, kind of, but it's not what you think."

She looked at his gorgeous eyes. She saw something in them she had never seen before. It looked like sadness, not the joy she was feeling right now.

"Babe," he said, reaching across the table and taking her gnarled hands in his. She felt so self-conscious now. Her hands were rough from her daily duties. His were soft as a baby, but she held on. She held on for dear life.

"Your news is you got a job, right?" she asked hesitantly.

"Yes, I did. But that is only part of the news," he said somewhat sheepishly.

"Then what is the other part of the news? It's good news, isn't it? Just tell me. I want to know why you're being so distant. You're acting weird, honey. Tell me."

"I got a job at a reasonable-sized law firm, but it's in New York."

"New York? Why there?" she asked.

"It's where I want to practice law. It's the job I've always wanted. I want to practice corporate law. This town just isn't big enough to have the cases I want to handle."

"But what about the store? I mean, if we move to New York, I'll have to sell the store. It could take months to sell and move up there. When are you starting this job?"

"Two months," he said, looking down at his plate. "They're setting up a new division, and it will take about two months."

"Two months? That's not enough time for me to settle things here. And you should have discussed it with me. I'm not even sure if I want to move to New York. I grew up here in Bridgeton. Even if I wanted to go, I couldn't pack up and leave that quickly. I have Jaime and Reilly, who depend on me for their jobs. Can't you find a job here?" she said.

"No. I can't. There are no firms here that do that kind of work. And to be honest, you wouldn't like it in New York."

"I guess I can shut the store for a few days, and we could go so I could at least get a feel for the city."

"No. That wouldn't be a good idea. You wouldn't like it there. Really, you wouldn't," he countered.

"That's why you haven't talked to me. You went to New York last week. Didn't you?"

"Yes. They wanted a face-to-face interview."

"Without even telling me? You applied and kept me in the dark! You didn't want me to know about it!"

"I didn't think you would want to go. You have a store to run. Besides, you wouldn't fit in with those kinds of people," he said in defense.

"What do you mean... those kinds of people? What kind of people are they?"

"You know. High society. They deal with the upper financial levels of people. You may feel out of place. I'm just looking out for your feelings."

"Looking out for me? You don't want me around your new associates. You're embarrassed to be with me. Aren't you? I look funny. I talk funny because of my cerebral palsy," she said, raising her voice.

"Shush. Lower your voice. People are looking at us!" he said sternly.

She glared back at him. "Why should I? Are you now embarrassed to be seen with the people here in Bridgeton? Listen, you little weasel, I know many of the people in this restaurant. They're my customers."

She turned around and began speaking to some of the other people. "Hello, Margaret." She nodded to Margaret's husband sitting beside her. "Hi, Harold. How are the grandchildren doing? The oldest will graduate from Bridgeton High this spring, won't he?"

Harold smiled and nodded in agreement.

She continued around the dining area. "Hi, Larry and Mary. I see you're on a date night. Good for you. It's always good to take some time for yourselves. Jenny and Richard, I see you ordered Pasta Fazioli. It's good. Isn't it? I knew you'd like it. If I remember correctly, it's your fiftieth wedding anniversary, isn't it?" She continued calling out several more names as she circled the room. "Now, Kevin, you have their attention. Please tell everyone that you invited me here to tell me you are leaving and moving to New York. Tell them you are embarrassed to be seen with me. Tell them, Kevin! After all I have done for you."

Kevin sat bolt upright. He blushed red crimson but remained silent.

Sassy continued. She called out again. "To my friends and customers, I thought he and I were in love. He quit his job. I put him through law school by working in my little store. Now he's embarrassed to have me with him and his high-class new employers. I'm no longer good enough for him."

All eyes were on Kevin, and they were all glaring with loathing. One man got up, walked over to Sassy and gave her a hug.

Luigi came over and said, "Mr. Kevin, you are no longer allowed in my restaurant. Pay your bill and get out. Leave now before I have you thrown out!"

Another man got up and laid a one-hundred-dollar bill on the table and said to Kevin. "You are not good enough to pay for her meal, you jerk!"

Kevin slowly got out of his seat and started to leave. Sassy called him back. "Where are you going?"

"I'm leaving," he said sheepishly.

"How?" she asked.

"In my car," he answered sheepishly.

"You mean, my car, don't you? It's titled in my name. Hand over the keys!"

He stood motionless.

"I said, give them to me. NOW! The apartment you are living in. It's in my name. Give me the keys!" she said with her hand out.

He continued to stand motionless. Suddenly, someone grabbed his shoulder. A voice said calmly from behind him. "Hand her the keys, Kevin."

As the person began to squeeze his shoulder, he winced. "Okay." He reached in his pocket and took out a keyring of keys and handed it to her outstretched hand.

"Oh. Yes. You have my credit card. I want that also," she added.

"But my name is on it. You can't even use it."

"I'm the primary account holder. I just revoked your charging ability on my account. Hand it over."

The hand tightened on his shoulder, and he reached into his back pocket for his wallet.

When he gave her the credit card, she smiled, nodded and said, "Now you can leave, you little worm."

As he walked out, someone in the far corner of the room called to her. "I'll call my tow truck driver and have it towed to my dealership, and I'll have it re-keyed for you. No charge, Sassy."

Everyone in the room clapped as he left. One of her frequent customers insisted she sit with them.

As each party throughout the room finished their dinner, they came over and gave her a hug. Everyone wished her good luck. Some even said she was fortunate he was gone.

The ones who had insisted on her sitting with them took her home and made sure she was safely in her apartment. She sobbed as she slogged her way up the stairs that night and cried herself to sleep.

CHAPTER THREE

The following morning, she called Jaime and Reilly and told them to take the day off. She wasn't feeling well today. At around ten the following morning, Mickey Ray started pounding on her door, and he didn't stop until she came and unlocked it to let him in.

Mickey put his arms around her and hugged Sassy tightly. "I heard about what Kevin did to you. I'm so sorry. How can I help?" he said as he held her.

She cried again, and slowly garbled, "Nothing. You can't do anything, Mickey. I hurt so badly. I don't know what I'll do."

"As difficult as it may seem, you will get past this. I promise," he said soothingly, continuing to hold her to his chest.

Sassy continued to cry until she had no more tears and almost collapsed on the couch in the back room. Mickey had never been past the front of the store until now. At the back of the store was a stockroom. Set up in a corner of the room was a living room and break room for employees and guests that came for brief visits. The building was a turn of the last century store and gas station. It had gas pumps outside and a convenience store on the first level. Her apartment on the second floor had two bedrooms, a kitchen, a bathroom, and a small sitting room.

They were in the breakroom area, and Mickey waited for Sassy to compose herself. "I'm so sorry to have acted like a fool, Mickey. What did you hear about last night?"

"One of my employees was having dinner at Luigi's last night when you stood up and showed what an ass Kevin was to you. Believe me, he deserved the reaction he got from the other dinner customers."

"I feel humiliated."

"Don't be. Everyone who knows you is on your side. Do you need anything? How can I help you?"

She took the tissue Mickey handed her and dried her eyes. "There is nothing you can do for me, Mickey. You are a good friend."

"Do you need any money?" he asked.

"No, but I will have more now that I will no longer be supporting that jackass. I loved him so much. Now I just wish he would die!" she said.

Mickey couldn't help laughing. "No, you don't wish that. But I completely understand your feelings. Here's my cell number," he said as he took a business card out of his wallet and wrote a number on the back.

"You can call this number anytime. Day or night. Just don't do anything stupid," he said.

"Like what?" she asked, surprised at his question.

"Well, you know...." he said hesitantly. "Matters of the heart can be very powerful. It makes people do stupid things. I mean seriously stupid things."

"Yeah, but I'm not suicidal, if that's what you mean. I won't do anything stupid like that," she said, still sniffling.

"Promise me?"

"I promise. Cross my heart and hope to die," she said, wrinkling her nose and crossing her heart with a gnarled hand.

"Nope. Don't hope to die," he laughed. He leaned over, took her hand and clasped it in his hands. "I'll help you get through this. I promise to be here when you need me. If I remember correctly, he lives in one of my apartments, doesn't he?"

She nodded her head, and sniffled, "Yes. He does. I've been paying his rent and utilities since he moved in for over two years."

"Well, that stops now. You will stop paying his rent."

"But the lease is in my name, so I have to pay it."

"Not anymore. Your lease is officially canceled. You owe me nothing. I'll send Kevin an eviction notice, effective immediately."

"But legally, you can't do that. Don't you have to have cause to cancel a lease?"

"First, as you pointed out, the lease is in your name. He is not a legal occupant. He is there with your permission. You rescind that permission. A tenant can move out and break a lease without reason as long as they give notice. Since that is so, in theory a landlord can do the same. I may have to check into that to make sure. But no matter what, we can figure out something. My dad plays golf with the mayor and the city attorney. Kevin Samson doesn't have a chance."

"But now he is a lawyer, he can fight it."

"True, but he is an inexperience lawyer. My attorneys are the best real estate attorneys in the state."

She looked up at him. "I don't deserve a friend like you, Mickey Ray Christianson."

"It is my pleasure to be your friend, Sassy." He smiled at her and went out the front door, gently closing it behind him.

Sassy thought to herself. "Why couldn't Kevin be more like Mickey?"

CHAPTER FOUR

When she opened the store a couple of days later, customers lined up for gas, coffee, and other items. The store was busy all day long. When she closed and turned off the pumps, everyone was exhausted. Jaime and Reilly were still willing to stay and stock the store for the next day.

All the customers were very kind. Many of them, as they paid for their items, refused to take their change. "Keep the change" was the topic of the day. She was still shocked from the other night and totally emotionally drained, but the outpouring of kindness and love from the residents of Bridgeton was amazing. It was busy the following week before things tapered off and went back to their normal days. Mickey Ray stopped by twice to check on her. Once, he even joined in and helped to wait on customers.

As things slowed down, she needed to order new stock to replenish the rapidly dwindling stock on the shelves. She needed to make a call to the supplier. Glenda Cunningham was an older woman and was the owner and manager of the supply house her parents used. Sassy used to call and place orders with Glenda when she was just a teenager and helped in the store after school.

"Hello, Sassy," Glenda responded when she answered the phone. "I've been expecting your call. I heard about what happened last week at Luigi's. I never liked Kevin. I'm glad he's gone."

Sassy took a deep breath as she answered, "Thanks, Glenda. I guess I made a fool of myself, but everyone in town has been wonderful to me. Their business and support have made things much better."

"Oh no, dear. You did no such thing. He deserved to be shown up for what he is. He's a no-good SOB!" Glenda said.

"I guess gossip is the disadvantage of living in a small town," Sassy added.

"Yeah, you're right, but it also has its advantages, like people stepping up to help. Did you know that your little store was one of the first in Bridgeton? The Browns, the ones that first opened it, were there for over fifty years. They were the first to have gas pumps in town. When they retired, they sold the business to Jackson O'Leary and his wife. They raised four boys in the little apartment upstairs where you live now. They retired and sold it to your mom and dad. Your mom and dad upgraded the whole place inside and out. They installed those self-service gas pumps."

"I knew Dad had the new pumps installed, but I didn't know all that history of this place," Sassy said politely.

"Yep, that place is a landmark in this town, Sassy. Now, what can I do for you this morning?"

"After we closed last night, Reilly stayed and took inventory. I'll email the order to you. I just called to see when I could get delivery. We've been so busy all week, we were too tired to place an order each day."

"I understand, dear. Don't you worry for a minute about it. I'll see if we can fast-track your order. How's Josh working out for you? He tells me he really likes you. I was wondering why he came back late on the night he delivers to you. He told me he stays to help you stock the shelves."

"Yes, he's really a nice guy," Sassy said.

"He's the only driver who has helped anyone stock their shelves. Usually they drop their load, and book out of there to get back to the warehouse," answered Glenda.

"I know, he's the only one that has done that for me either. Jaime just loves Josh. He's so sweet to her."

"Yep, he's a good egg," sighed Glenda.

"Thanks. We really need the stock. Let me know when it's loaded on the truck, so I'll be here."

"Sure will, darlin'. You take care now. And good luck."

"Okay. I will," Sassy said and hung up the phone. She smiled to herself. Glenda was her parents' age and still addressed her on the phone like she did when she was a child calling in orders. Glenda was a typical Southern lady.

She turned, and Reilly and Jaime were waiting for her to get off the phone.

"What do you want us to do?" asked Jaime with a serious, deadpan face. Reilly, as usual, stood silently, waiting for instructions.

"Reilly, you work on the books to get them in order. We'll be getting a shipment sometime later today or early tomorrow. Jaime, let's get this place cleaned up. We need to mop floors, dust the shelves, and rearrange things so we can effectively rotate the stock. Jaime, make a fresh pot of coffee. Let's move, people!"

They both moved into action without a word and spent the rest of the day between customers cleaning the store. As they were cleaning, the phone rang.

Jaime answered it and heard a screaming voice at the other end of the line. Jaime's face went pale. She looked at Sassy with the phone in her hand.

Sassy instantly recognized the voice. It was Kevin. She reached out to Jaime and told her it was okay. Jaime got upset when someone was angry with her, and she didn't always understand the nature of people.

When Sassy took the phone, she immediately said into the receiver, "Hey, Kevin! Calm down. You have no need or right to yell at Jaime. You know her very well, and you know how things like that upset her."

"I don't care how much it upsets her. I got an eviction notice from the rental office. What's going on, Sas?"

"You're living in my apartment, and I want you to leave," she answered.

"I know my rights. You can't do that. You have to give me proper notice. This letter tells me to be out by the weekend. That's the day after tomorrow!" he continued to scream into the phone at her.

"Kevin, the lease on the apartment is in my name, not yours. I pay the rent for it. You have been my guest. Not anymore. You must get out by the weekend," she said adamantly.

"Look you little witch, I will not get out. I will stay here for two months. The law says I must be given two months' notice to leave. So, I'm staying here for two more months or until I move to New York, whichever comes first, and there is nothing you can do about it."

"Get out by the weekend, or I will have the management change the locks," she said and slammed the phone down.

Jaime had been standing there just watching her talk to Kevin. "He sounded really mad at you. Did you do something to him, Sassy?" she asked.

"No. I didn't," Sassy said as she began to tear up. She felt awful. She wanted to cry, but she had a business to run, and it might upset Jaime if she broke down now. "Let's call it a day, guys. Put your cleaning stuff away, and you can go home," she said to them.

Reilly spoke up first. "It's not time to leave yet. We need to work until it's time to leave."

Jaime nodded in agreement. "Yeah. We want to do what's right. That is work until it is time to go home."

Sassy smiled at both. "I'm not feeling well, so you can go home early. We can close the store early today."

Reilly said, "Okay," and began shutting down the register.

Jaime came over to Sassy and hugged her. "I'm sorry you don't feel good. I wish I could make you feel better."

She removed a tear from her eye and turned to Jaime. "You make me feel better every day. Go home and have a good night. I will be fine."

She helped them shut down the store and locked the door when they both left. She went upstairs to her apartment. With the stress of Kevin's breakup, her cerebral palsy took control, and her body ached all over. She dropped onto the bed fully clothed and cried herself to sleep again.

CHAPTER FIVE

The next morning, she called Mickey's number on the back of his business card. Mickey answered, "Hello, Sassy. How are you? What can I do for you?"

"Oh, Mickey. Kevin called the store yesterday. He said he got an eviction notice."

"Yes. I had the resident manager do it. We are canceling your lease effective immediately. But your rent is paid until the end of the month. If you need the money, I will have accounting refund the balance of the month, as well as your security deposit."

"You don't need to do that. I don't mind if he stays until the end of the month. He says you can't do that. He says he has a right to a sixty-day notice."

"Yeah, technically, he's right, but it is your unit, and you have been paying the rent, so it's yours, and in certain cases you can require him to move out. It is a sticky rule, but we can push it to the limit. You don't need to worry about that. At the end of this week, I will have maintenance change the locks, but it will look better if you move into the unit. That will give you rights that may override his. Can you move?"

"I don't know if I can find someone to move my stuff that quickly."

"I'll check with our building manager and see if we have some men who can help you with that after we change the locks."

"Thanks, Mickey. One more thing. His car belongs to me too. He needed it to go to classes and stuff. The loan, title and insurance are all in my name. I don't go out much, so I don't really need a car, but when he leaves, I'm still responsible for it, and I'm making payments on it too. I got the keys, and I had Charles, the cab driver, bring it home for me."

"That, I don't know. I would assume that since everything is associated with it, including the title, you should be able to take immediate possession of it. Things like that are personal items, and you don't have to give notice to get your own car back. I'll talk to my sister, Darcy, and have her help you with some details of this mess."

She went downstairs and opened the store for the day. Mickey had stopped by and informed her that Darcy would help her get Kevin out of her apartment. He was having his lawyers investigate the entire situation. Maybe they could get some of the money back she had given him over the time he was in law school.

"That would be great, Mickey Ray. Do you think they can really recover some of my money?"

"To be honest, the attorney says he'll try, but it's a very slim chance. Since it was a gift, and you willingly gave it to him, you may not get it back. Since he has nothing, as the old saying goes, you can't get blood from a turnip. Even if you get some type of legal judgement, he can declare bankruptcy, and the debt goes away."

"I feel like such a fool. I swear, Mickey, I'll never fall in love again," she said sadly.

"This too will pass. You'll get over Kevin and fall in love again. I had a woman I fell in love with try to kill me," he said, almost laughing.

"Really?"

"Yep," he said.

As a customer came inside, got a loaf of bread, and a quart of milk, she rang it up when the phone rang. She asked Jaime to ring up the customer, and she answered the phone.

"You know I need a car to move my stuff. If I'm going to find another place to live, I need transportation to move my stuff out."

Sassy looked over at Mickey and then said into the phone, "That is my car, not yours, and how you move your stuff out is not my concern."

"How do you expect me to even function without funds? You took my credit card and locked our joint checking account yesterday. I can't do anything. You're being unreasonable."

His tone and attitude were working against her. She was getting red-faced with anger during Kevin's tirade. "Listen, you little worm!" she called into the phone. "I have supported you for the last two years.

You have contributed nothing to this relationship. The apartment is in my name because you have no job. I bought the car because you have no job, and our checking account and credit cards are all mine."

"I'll file an injunction against you. I'll take everything you own for doing this to me. You did it without consulting me or giving me any notice."

"You can go to hell," she yelled back. "If you get near me or anything that belongs to me, I'll kill you, Kevin Samson! Do you hear me? I'll shoot you dead! Don't mess with me!"

Mickey reached over and took the phone from her and put it to his ear. "Kevin, this conversation is over. You will not come here or anywhere near her or anything that belongs to her. Because of your actions now, she will get a restraining order against you." He then calmly placed the phone back on the cradle.

She was upset and crying again. Mickey pulled her close and stroked her hair as he held her against his chest as she cried. "He's constantly texting me. He calls me at all hours of the day and at night. I had to turn off my cell phone. The phone in the store is tied up with his calls."

The customer who was at the register saw and heard the entire conversation. The woman shook her head in sympathy and walked out the door. Jaime stood blank-faced, looking at both Sassy and Mickey as he comforted Sassy.

As Sassy calmed down, Mickey got a tissue and wiped tears from her face. He pulled back and said to her. "Darcy will be here later. She will help you make all the arrangements to take possession of your apartment. She will also have our attorney get a restraining order. The Christianson Company will assist you through the entire process."

Sassy silently nodded her head and sniffled, trying to control her emotions.

"Let's go out and look at your car," Mickey said.

They walked out, and they each walked around it. It was a two-year-old Honda Accord.

"It doesn't look too bad. At least he took care of it," stated Mickey.

"Yeah, with my money. I made the payments, and every time it needed service, I paid for it," she said sadly.

"Can you drive?" Mickey asked.

"I think so. I used to drive, and I have a license, but I haven't driven at all since I bought this one for Kevin. He took me to most places I needed to go when he could. If he wasn't available, then Charles took me."

"Who is Charles?" asked Mickey.

"He's a driver for the Bridgeton Yellow Cab Company. We went to school together. He was two years ahead of me and kind of looked out for me back then and sometimes still does even now."

"That's very nice of him. I've got to go to work now. Just hang in until Darcy Jean gets here. We'll talk more later, Sas." Mickey left her standing beside the car.

She went inside and got the extra set of keys. Back outside, she opened the door and got in the driver's seat. She had always sat in the passenger seat. She put the key in the ignition and started the engine. It felt good to feel the engine running. She slowly put it into gear and moved the car forward about ten feet, then backed it up. That was enough for now. Maybe she would slowly relearn how to drive, but not today. She got out, locked the door and went back inside to help Jaime and Reilly.

Later that day, Darcy Jean Bower, Mickey Ray's sister, came by and did as he promised. Kevin's earlier phone call still rattled Sassy. Darcy told her to carry on as usual, and she would make calls to their attorney.

"Darcy, I loved him so much. He totally caught me off guard when he told me he didn't want me to go with him," she said.

"I know. Men can be such asses sometimes," Darcy commented. "You'll get through it. I promise."

"I just wish he would die. If he did, at least it would be over, and I wouldn't have to go through all this crap from him."

"I know. You're going through what many couples go through in a divorce situation. It'll all be over soon enough."

They talked for a while, and Darcy left with an entire list of things she needed to do to settle this situation. Meanwhile, since it was getting late in the afternoon, Jaime and Reilly prepared to close the store.

CHAPTER SIX

assy hadn't talked to her parents for over a week. She usually talked to them every couple of days, but in the small town of Bridgeton, she knew her parents knew what happened at Luigi's. She just didn't feel like facing them. They were wonderful parents, and they would fully support her, but she felt like such a fool.

"Oh, well," she thought to herself. "I have to face them sometime," she said out loud. She called the taxi service and again requested Charles. When Charles pulled up in his cab and honked his horn, she headed for the door.

Charles had been her driver of choice since she sold her car to help pay for Kevin's tuition. She had been certified to drive even with her disability, but now that she no longer had a car, she took a cab everywhere. Because she owned the convenience store, and many needed items could be delivered, she rarely needed to drive. Bridgeton was so small it didn't have an Uber service. The small cab company had been in business for many years, but was down to only a very few drivers, and most of them were only part time. Charles Townsend had driven a cab since he got out of high school.

She told Charlie she wanted to go to her parent's house. He turned around to her and saw the sadness in her eyes. "I heard about what happened at Luigi's. What did your mom and dad say when you told them about Kevin?"

"I haven't talked to them since it happened. Maybe they don't know yet."

"Sassy, you should have at least called them," he said.

"I know, Charles. When I don't call them, they know I'm upset about something, and they just let me work it out. They're wonderful parents and leave me alone when I need it."

"I see. I'm like a mobile bartender. You can talk to me if you ever need a shoulder to cry on. I know you don't drink, but look in that cooler on the floor. There's a small selection of soft drinks in it. Take one and talk about it as I drive. I'll take the long way to your mom and dad's house. The ride's on me today, Sassy."

She laid her head back on the seat's headrest and looked up. "Thanks, Charles. I need a little time to vent."

Charles slowly drove into the sparse traffic, driving as smoothly and slowly as he could. He reached up and shut the meter off.

She said nothing as he drove. He looked in his rearview mirror and saw tears running from her eyes. His heart ached for her. She was such a sweet person, and he hated Kevin had treated her like he did. He wanted her to have some time to herself as he drove. As a cab driver, he knew that sometimes people wanted to talk. Other times, they wanted people around but still wanted to be alone with their thoughts. Right now, this was Sassafras Magill. He drove to the other side of town and turned onto a side road that led to the public park and lake. It was late in the afternoon, and few people would be there. He drove to a parking area near the lake.

Charles parked, got out, opened the door and helped Sassy get out. He handed her a tissue without a word. She wiped her eyes as she started toward the lake. Charles followed a few feet behind, giving her a sense of being alone.

Her walk was a bit wobbly, but her smile would bring happiness to any crowd of people. Her kindness to those she met made people immediately comfortable around her. Sassy walked, and she cried. Charles felt her sadness. On the other side of the lake was a park bench. She walked to it and sat at one end and looked out at the water.

"Charles, please come around and sit with me," she said. He moved around and sat at the other end of the bench. He still said nothing.

Finally, she spoke to him, never taking her eyes off the water. "I loved him, you know."

He didn't answer. It was a statement that needed no answer.

"I would have died for him. I gave him every bit of extra money I earned for the last few years to put him through law school. Did you know that?"

"No. I didn't. Until the other night, I didn't think anyone in town knew what you were doing for him."

"How foolish I was to love a man so much."

"Love is sometimes blind, Sassy."

"Blind, and stupid," she said as a new flow of tears flowed down her cheeks. "I never slept with him, you know."

"That's admirable," he answered.

"I just wanted to remain pure. I wanted to wait until we were married. Make that part so special. "

Now he was getting somewhat out of his comfort zone. He had never had a conversation about sex with a woman before. He made no comment about that remark.

"I guess maybe that's why he didn't love me enough to want me to go with him."

"I'm sure that had nothing to do with it."

"Sex is very important to men."

Now he was getting a little embarrassed. "Yes, it is, but a man should respect a woman with her personal um...you know...personal actions."

She turned and smiled for the first time since she had gotten into his cab this evening. "Personal actions, Charles? Really? That's your response?"

"Yeah. Hey I don't get into talks about sex with women. Especially a beautiful lady like you, Sassy!"

Her smile disappeared just as quickly as it had come. "Beautiful? You think I'm beautiful?" she asked, showing him her gnarled hands. "I'm messed up. I'm broken. I'm handicapped. Have you looked at me lately, Charles?"

He also straightened up and looked her straight into her eyes. "I will listen to you cry. I will hand you dry tissues, but I will NOT sit here and listen to you degrade yourself because you won't have sex with a man. Any man, and I mean any man, who thinks less of a woman that refuses to have sex with him because she's waiting for it to be special on their wedding day, is not worthy of her love. And that goes for Kevin too. Kevin is a horrible, selfish man. He would have done the same thing if you had slept with him. That's not why he didn't want you to go with him. He's a — I don't know the proper words to even describe him, Sassy. Don't you ever put yourself down like that again."

"Well then, what's wrong with me? Why doesn't he want me? It has to be because of my handicap. Why was I born like this, Charles? Why?"

He slid across the bench to her and put his arm around her in a friendly way and pulled her close, like a brother. "I don't know why you were born like you are, but you are a very special person. I promise you that."

"Do you really think so?" she cried. "As much as I loved him, now I hate him. I've been paying the rent for the apartment he lives in. I gave him a car and fully supported him. Now he's harassing me because I refuse to continue giving him money. I want him to move out of the apartment that I'm paying for. How mean and cruel is that?" she stated.

"Someday you will meet a person who loves you despite your condition. It won't matter to him," Charles said as he stroked her hair.

"I promise. It will happen. When you meet someone, fall in love and get married, just remember that a poor, dumb cab driver told you it would happen. You have my word that it will happen."

She buried her face in his chest and cried again. "I hope you're right, but right now, I wish he was dead. If he was, I could be free and move on. I want him to leave me alone."

In a few minutes, again her eyes were empty of tears. He slowly moved her away from him. "Come on, let's get your face cleaned up."

He got up, took a handkerchief out of his pocket, and walked to the lake and dipped it into the cool, clear water. He wrung it out as he walked back to the bench.

Then he wiped off her face, and raised her head to look at him. "Let's wash away these tears. Put on your confident face, and let your parents know you're glad that Kevin, that financial cancer, is gone. He's out of your life forever."

She sniffled a few times as he continued to wipe her face.

They walked back to his cab, and he drove to her parents' home.

He got out and opened the door for her to get out. As she exited the vehicle, he said to her, "Now, hold your head high, and be the proud, confident woman you are." He looked at her with a smile. "Okay, you don't feel confident and proud, but you can pretend."

She forced a smile. "Okay, Charles."

"Great. What time do you want me to pick you up?" he asked.

"What time does your shift end?" she asked shakily.

"For you, it never ends," he answered as he walked her to the door and rang the bell.

When her mother answered the door, Charles said to her, "A very special delivery for you, Mrs. Magill."

She smiled at him. "Thank you, Charles. How is your family?"

"Mom and Dad are doing fine. Thanks for asking," he answered.

"When you see them, tell them we missed them at church last Sunday."

"I'll do that, Mrs. Magill," he said as he turned, and waved goodbye.

"Come on in, Sassy. I fixed your favorite dinner tonight, honey," she said, putting her arms around Sassy and giving her a hug.

"Oh, good. I haven't had spaghetti since the last time you fixed it for me. It's so messy for me to eat," she said with a laugh.

She rarely ate spaghetti because her hands would shake when she ate. Most of the time she made such a mess when it fell off her fork. She would usually cut it up so she could eat it with a spoon. If she planned on eating something messy in public, she would ask for a large napkin or carry a bib in her purse.

"Your dad's in the living room. I'll be there in just a few minutes. I'm warming up the sauce now. I'll come get you when it's ready," her mother said.

Sassy hugged her dad and sat down in a stuffed chair. The living room was tastefully decorated with comfortable deep-stuffed chairs and a couch. Around the room were a variety of pictures of Sassy at various ages. Anyone coming into this room would immediately see the love her parents had for their only daughter.

"Well, Daddy, what have you been up to this week?" she asked.

"Nothing much. Your mom and I drove down to Williamsburg to the outlets and did some shopping. You know she loves to shop. I think she even picked up a few things for you."

"Yes, Mom loves to shop. And she knows I have way more clothes than I can wear. I don't need more," she laughed.

"You don't need more of what, dear?" her mother said, walking into the room as she wiped her hands on a dishcloth.

"I don't need more clothes, Mom."

"Dinner's ready. That's not the point. I got you something that will look stunning on you. We heard what happened between you and Kevin. You need some new clothes when you date again."

"Oh, Mom, let's not get into that. Not now. Please?"

"Leave her alone, Alice. She'll talk to us when she's ready," her father said, getting up from his chair. "Let's eat," he said, walking toward the dining room.

The dining room was small, with a table and six chairs. On the walls were pictures with scenes of forests and wildlife, and one wall had a picture of a bowl of fruit. The opposite wall had a print of a family bowed in prayer at a dinner table.

Her father took Sassy's hand, and her mother, sitting across the table from her father, took Sassy's other hand. They all bowed, and he asked for a blessing on dinner.

As he said amen, he raised his head and put a napkin on his lap. "Other than that awful situation at Luigi's last week, what else have you been doing? How's business at the store?"

"It has been doing very well. Since that incident, everyone has shown their support. They stop by, fill their gas tanks, and pick up lots of simple odds and ends at the store," she answered as she cut up the spaghetti. "Charlie, the cab driver, stops by to fill up several times a week. There are some gas stations that are cheaper than mine, but he supports me. He usually gives me a discount on my fare and refuses to take a tip."

"That's good. I'm glad to hear that. The people in this town really come together when they feel one of us has had a rough time."

"I know, Daddy. They are great people here. Just give me some space. I'll get myself together. I just need some time. Please."

"Okay. Can I at least ask you a couple of questions, Sas?" her father asked gently.

"What questions?"

"If I understand correctly, you gave him money to pay his college tuition?"

"Yes, I did, Daddy. He promised that when he graduated, passed the bar, and got a job, we would get married. Then money wouldn't be a problem."

"And you are not getting married. Correct?"

"That's right, Daddy. He's moving to New York to take a position there as a litigation attorney."

"Is he going to pay that money back?"

"We didn't specifically discuss it, but I doubt it. It was a gift. Not officially a loan, so he has no legal obligation to pay it back."

"Are you going to at least look into it?"

"Yes, I will look into it, Daddy. Now let's not talk about it anymore. Let's play a game of cards."

"That sounds good. I'll get the cards," her mother said as she cleared the table of dishes. After a couple of hours, it was late, and her father took her home to save her cab fare. She was home before eleven o'clock.

CHAPTER SEVEN

The following morning, Detective Halligan stood over the body, then looked around at the scene. The man at his feet had been bludgeoned to death by a rock that was lying two feet from the body. He directed the officers to put the yellow crime scene tape around the scene in a 20-foot circle from the waterline of the lake and asked who had found the body.

"He was found by an early morning jogger. He says he jogs this route three to four times a week," the officer answered, pointing to a man standing off to the side of the cordoned-off area.

The crime scene was at the city park down by the lake. A few feet from the body was a wrought-iron bench placed there so people could look out over the water, and sometimes feed the wildlife that came around. With all the commotion there now, the ducks and geese kept circling near the shore, hoping for a handout. The officers kept shooing them away from the shore to keep them from trampling all over the open ground.

A dozen or more officers had taken up guard positions. Forensic personnel wearing blue coveralls and footies over their shoes carefully walked the area. They were looking for anything they could remove, analyze and connect with the crime. A man snapped pictures of the area in a grid pattern to assemble later on a board at the police station.

Detective Halligan, also wearing the blue footies, went over and bent over the body to ask the coroner, "Can you give me a TOD?"

The coroner answered, "An estimate of time of death would be between 11 PM and 2 AM. I'll take a liver temp, and that might give us a tighter time. Also, I need to check the air temperature during that time, so we can calculate it. I assume he was killed here, but I need to check blood lividity before I can say for sure."

Detective Halligan, still leaning over, said, "I'm sure he was killed here. I don't think someone would kill the victim, drag his body here, and then place the murder weapon right beside the body."

Without even looking up from his work, the doctor stated, "Stranger things have happened. I'll give you my report later when I get him back to the morgue. Now, if you don't mind, leave me alone to complete my work."

Halligan turned to one of the forensic technicians and said, "Be sure to check that bench over there for prints."

"Will do," the technician answered, "but this is a public bench. There are probably a million sets of prints on it."

"Just do it!" Halligan ordered.

The tech continued working without a word.

Halligan straightened his coat and walked away mumbling, "I should never have transferred here. I should have stayed in New York. I thought things would be slower here in this Podunk town."

The supply truck rolled up, Josh got out and started wheeling in the new stock. Jaime, Reilly and Sassy were at the front of the store waiting on customers as he wheeled his hand truck in through the back door.

"Okay," he said as he slid the items off the bottom of the hand truck. He returned to the truck, brought another load, and continued until he had placed the entire order inside, in the middle of the store. Customers had to wind through the stacked boxes to make their purchases. Josh began cutting boxes open and handing items to Jaime and Reilly as they put them on the shelves.

After a lull between customers, Sassy joined in and helped stock the shelves. In just a few minutes, there was nothing left but empty boxes. Josh began using a box cutter to break down the boxes and then took them out to the trash dumper. Finally, everything was put on the shelves, and they all sat down to take a break.

"Well, ladies and gentlemen," Josh said as he made a mock salute toward them, another round of restocking complete. Business has really picked up for you, Sassy. You should order more often so your shelves don't get empty. You could lose money when you don't have what people want."

She sighed. "You're right. Things have been topsy-turvy since what happened the other night."

"I heard about that. I'm so sorry to hear that happened," he said.

Reilly turned and went back to the computer terminal and prepared to enter the new stock items into the inventory database. Jaime went to another part of the store to sweep up the dust and dirt.

"Yeah, I guess people break up and make up all the time," Sassy said.

He moved closer to Sassy. "That's true, but not after what you did to help him so much."

"He's gone now, so need to move forward, and not let it bother me too much," she said.

"Who's car is that sitting beside the store?" he asked.

"It's mine," answered Sassy.

"I didn't know you had a car. I've never seen it before. Someone brought it here yesterday."

"Yes. I bought it for Kevin. And I took it back the other day."

"You gave him a car?" he asked.

"Yeah. I know. It was stupid, but I did."

"Don't let it bother you. We all do stupid things sometimes. I have done similar things."

"Like what?" Sassy asked.

"It's not important. We all need to move on. That's what brought me here to Bridgeton. I'm originally from out west. This was as far away from my problems as I could get. When we love, and lose, we all end up a bit broken. Don't you think?"

"I guess so. But sometimes it hurts so much."

He shrugged. "I know. Tell me about it. I can relate."

"How can you relate, Josh?"

He smiled. "It's not worth mentioning. Hey, I have to get the truck back and get it cleaned up for my morning run tomorrow."

"I don't want to hold you up more than we already have. Thanks again for helping us stock the shelves. Jaime and Reilly really like you."

"I like them too. Gotta go. See you in a few days. Don't wait so long between orders. It's easier to unload and stock. Also, I get to see you more often," he said with a wink.

When he was gone, Jamie said to Sassy. "He's nice."

"Yes, he is," Sassy answered.

"Kevin never talked to me."

"Sure he did," Sassy said.

"No, he didn't. He would only talk to me when he wanted me to get you. I don't think he liked me."

"Why do you say that?" Sassy asked.

"I told you. He never talked to me. He never said hello or goodbye. He never said to have a good day. Nothin," answered Jaime.

"Yeah. I guess he didn't. I never realized that," Sassy said reflectively. "He really wasn't very nice to either of you, was he?"

"No," said Jaime.

It was an uneventful day until the police arrived that afternoon. "Are you Sassafras Magill?" the officer asked her.

She looked at him. "Of course, Bill. You've known me for most of your life." She knew instinctively that something was seriously wrong. "Why are you here, and why are you asking my name?"

"Sorry Sas. I had to ask. I have to ask you to come with me down to the station for questioning."

"Okay. Why?" she asked.

"I'll explain on the way. There's been an incident we need to ask you about."

"What incident?"

"I can't say here. If you just explain it to Jaime and Reilly, we can go. Do you think they can take care of things until you get back?" he asked.

"Yeah. I guess they can look out for things for a while. Will it take long?"

"I don't really know how long it'll take. Do you want to call someone to come over in case it takes longer than you expect?"

"Yes, Bill, I'd like that. Do you mind if I call my dad?"

"Go ahead, but we can't wait until he gets here."

"I understand. Jaime and Reilly can take care of things until Daddy arrives. Let's go. I'd like to get back before the afternoon rush. Can I get my purse in the back room?"

"Yes. But hurry."

When Sassy went to the back room, Bill turned to Reilly. "Hey Reilly. How ya doin?"

"I'm fine, Officer Bill," he answered as he wiped off the counter area around the register.

"You always keep a clean floor, Jaime," Bill said, smiling at her.

"Thank you, Officer Bill," she answered with a returned smile.

"Every time I come in here, I tell you to call me just Bill, not Officer Bill."

She looked up at him and smiled. "I know."

Sassy came back out with her purse and followed Bill to his police car and got in the back seat. He knew he wasn't following police procedure and protocol, but in this small town of Bridgeton, everyone knew everyone else. He didn't need to make Sassafras feel any more uncomfortable that she was already feeling. It was the first time in her life she had ever ridden in a police car.

They arrived at the Bridgeton Police building, and Bill followed her inside and led her to an interrogation room. He asked her if she wanted something to drink and got her a soda from the machine in the officers' breakroom.

As he placed the soda can on the table, he said, "I'm really sorry about this, Sassy."

"Don't worry about it, Bill. I understand. And I also know that one reason you offered me a drink is so you can get my fingerprints from the can. I've never had a reason to be fingerprinted before, so they aren't in your system."

Bill looked at the floor and blushed. "Yeah. You're right. I'm just doing what I'm told."

She reached over and placed her hand on his as he gripped the table. "I know. You're a very sweet man. You're doing your job. Don't apologize. I've done nothing wrong, so whatever is going on here, I'll be gone in a few minutes." She firmly placed her hand around the soda can and squeezed.

She slid it over to Bill. "Here, I've tried to give you a good print. You can take it."

He continued to blush. "Thanks, Sassy. Can I get you another drink?"

"Not now. I'm fine. Say hello to your wife, Sue, tonight. When is the baby due?" she asked him.

"She still has another month. It's a boy, you know. We're both so happy." Now, he beamed with pride.

"I don't know who the luckiest person is, you or her. I hope both of you have a healthy baby boy," Sassy said, smiling.

Just then, the door opened, and a detective walked in. "Miss Magill?" he said, addressing her. "I'm Detective Halligan."

Bill turned and walked out of the room. She nodded and looked at the detective. "Good morning, sir. I don't know you."

He sat and looked at her and seriously answered, "I've only been here for a couple of months. I understand you are a fixture in this Podunk town, but that won't stop me from upholding the law here. The laws concerning murder are very serious everywhere."

"Okay, but I don't understand what any of this has to do with me," she said, getting a bit defensive.

"Someone killed Kevin Albert Samson last night in the Lakeside City Park. You and he had an altercation a few nights ago at Luigi's Italian Restaurant. Am I correct?" he asked.

"No. I didn't know. This is the first time I've heard of this. To answer your second question, yes. We had an argument. He broke up with me, and I told him off in front of the entire dinner crowd."

"You had given him quite a bit of money over the past couple of years. Am I correct about that fact also?" he continued.

Sassy felt the heat in the room rise. She gave a one-word answer. "Yes."

"That is what we call motive, Miss Magill," he said as his dark eyes bore into hers.

"You call it motive. I call it baloney. To charge me with something so ridiculous, I think you need means and opportunity."

"True, but we can hold you for forty-eight hours while we investigate and charge you," he said blandly.

"Lawyer," she said and sat back in the chair.

"If you're innocent, you don't need a lawyer," he said as he continued to glare at her.

"Lawyer!" she repeated.

"I see you're disabled, and he took a lot of money from you. You had a good reason to kill him. I sure would want to do that to someone who had cheated me."

For the third time, she repeated, "Lawyer."

"I'm just trying to help you, Miss Magill," he said.

She didn't answer, but she met his gaze with her own dark brown eyes.

Eye to eye, they stared silently, boring into each other's souls. Finally, he broke the visual connection, got up and walked out of the room.

She sat there for over an hour in the dead silence of the small stuffy room. It was hot, and she was getting sweaty. She also knew this was one method cops used on people they hoped would finally break down. Bill came back in with an ice-cold bottle of water.

He set the bottle on the table. "I'm so sorry about all this. Can I notify your family for you?"

"Thanks, Bill. Yes. Call my dad and tell him to call Darcy Jean Bower and tell her where I am, please. I should have called them before we left the store, but I didn't think I would end up here being held on suspicion of murder."

"I can do that for you." He left the room, and it was quiet once again. Later, the detective entered the room again, followed by another man carrying a briefcase.

When he entered, the detective left. The man came over and sat in front of her and introduced himself. "Hello, Miss Magill. I'm Patrick Donaldson. Darcy Bower contacted me. She asked me to represent you in this case. What have you told them so far?"

"Nothing. I didn't do anything. I don't know anything," she said, now losing her resolve and anger at the situation. "How much is this going to cost me? I don't have any money."

"Don't worry about that right now. We'll work that out later. It's good that you said nothing. Now tell me everything. Start with when you met Mr. Samson," he instructed.

It took over an hour before he exited the interview room and walked to Darcy, who had been patiently waiting outside.

"So how did it go?" Darcy asked.

"I think she is telling the truth."

"So, you don't think she killed Kevin?"

"It doesn't matter what I believe, Darcy. What matters is, can I get her off if she's charged?" he answered.

"Don't give me that crap. Do you believe her or not, Patrick?" she insisted.

He hesitated, then answered. "Yes. I believe her. I'm not positive, but I think she's innocent. They don't have any evidence. If they did, they'd have booked her, not just called her in for questioning. They'll have a full investigation. I'll talk to the detective. I'm sure they'll have to let her go at least until they find something that might tie her to his murder."

"Thanks, Patrick. I'll wait outside until you get all her paperwork done so I can take her home."

When Sassy came out, Darcy brought the car up front, so she didn't have as far to walk.

As Darcy drove, Sassy almost broke down again. "I was so scared back there. All I could think of was I didn't kill Kevin. I didn't want them to think I did, so I tried to be strong, and ask for a lawyer. Did I do the wrong thing? I didn't want them to know how scared I was. If I did act scared, maybe they would think I was guilty."

Darcy said, "You did the right thing. I don't really know how a guilty person would act, so I don't know about that, but asking for a lawyer was the right thing to do."

Darcy took her back to the store and went in to meet her father, who had been helping Jaime and Reilly with the store.

"Hello, Mr. Magill. It's nice to meet you and the Mrs. I've heard so much about you in the short time I've known Sassy," Darcy said as he rose from his chair behind the counter. Beside him was Sassy's mother. She also stood and shook hands.

"It's nice to meet you, Mrs. Bower," she said.

"Please, everyone calls me Dee," she said with a smile. "I'm sorry I must leave. I have a lot of things to do. We'll be seeing a lot of each other in the next few days. I'm going to find the person who killed Kevin, or at least prove Sassy didn't do it."

Darcy went back home instead of back to her office.

"James, I'm home. Where are you?"

"I'm in the office," he called back to her.

She walked into the office just as James clicked off the computer screen.

"Another mission?" she asked, knowing she couldn't ask for details.

"Yes, but I don't know if we'll take this one. It could take several weeks abroad, and I don't want to be gone that long from you and the kids. And Mickey is also busy with projects for the Christianson Company."

"Don't I know it! Between your missions, Mickey being with you, and work here, sometimes I don't see either of you for weeks at a time."

"How was your day?" he asked.

"Awful. Do you know that little store and gas station at the end of North Main Street?"

"The place across from the bank?" he asked.

That's South Main Street. The other end. The one owned by the girl with cerebral palsy."

"Oh, yeah. What about her?" he asked.

"Someone killed her boyfriend last night, and they think she may have done it because he took a lot of her money. They don't have any evidence to tie her to his murder, but she has a motive."

"And that affects us how?" he asked.

"I don't think she did it, and I'm going to find his killer."

"You have no experience in doing something like that. Please, Dee, don't get involved," he pleaded.

"I'm already involved. I promised her I would help her."

"You're just like your brother, Mickey Ray. You have this compulsion to help people!" he said.

"And that's a bad thing how?" she asked.

"I guess it's not bad. I'm going to Mickey's house for a while. Don't wait up," he said, getting up and heading out the door.

She logged onto her computer to answer some emails. After that, she showered and went to bed. She would have a busy day tomorrow.

CHAPTER EIGHT

The following morning, Darcy sat at her desk thinking about what had happened the day before to Sassafras. Everyone in town knew her and knew that she was a kind and gentle person. She would hurt no one, but it was true that sometimes even good people do bad things when they're pushed into a corner. Sassy felt betrayed and cheated by the person she had loved and supported.

Darcy intended to find out the truth about Kevin Samson, believing Sassy was innocent until evidence showed otherwise. She leaned over her desk and pushed a button on her intercom. "Monica, would you come to my office, please?"

Monica came in and sat down in the chair in front of Darcy. "What's the plan for the day, Darcy?"

"Did you hear about the murder in the city park the night before last?"

"Yes. I did. What about it?"

Darcy said, "I'm curious about Kevin Samson. I want to know more about him. Can you run a complete background check on him for me?"

"I can do that, but what connection do we have with him?" she asked.

"We have no connection to him. He lived in one of our apartments, but nothing other than that. I'm just curious about his past. Get everything on him you can."

"What priority do you want this to have? I have a lot of work piled on my desk right now," Monica said.

"Pass that work to some of your assistants. I want a background on Samson ASAP."

"Will do. I'll get on it now, but it may take me a while."

"I want a full check. Start with past employment and why he left them. Past residence, and why he moved, and what kind of tenant he was. Then dig into his personal life and his college background. I want to know the date and time he lost his virginity and who he lost it to. I want to know the names of every girlfriend since elementary school. If you can get it, I even want his medical background. Can you do that?" Darcy asked.

"I'll do my best, but the medical may be a bit more difficult. There are laws about that."

"He's dead, Monica. Once a person is dead, many of those laws no longer count. Do the best you can. I want it yesterday."

"Okay...it must be important for you to want all this information. May I ask why you need it?" she asked.

"Not yet. As soon as I can get more info on Samson, I'll bring you up to speed."

"Got it. I'll get right on it."

"Oh, one more thing. The easiest things should be his past employment and past residences. Get them to me as soon as you get it, please."

When Monica left, Darcy picked up the phone and dialed her best friend, Millicent.

"Hey, Millie. Are you up yet?" she asked.

Darcy knew that her friend sometimes slept until noon and stayed up half the night watching old black and white movies. Millie would get up, have pastries for breakfast and spend the next two hours at her home gym working off those calories. She had married and divorced an abusive man. In the settlement, she got the house and a settlement of ten million dollars. She was very attractive, loved male company and the men loved her, but marriage was no longer on the table for her foreseeable future. She was smart but a bit spacey. As some would describe her, Millicent was a mental blonde.

"I'm almost awake. What's the reason for calling so early, girlfriend?"

"Early? It's almost 8 o'clock," Darcy laughed.

"That's what I said.... early!" she said, yawning.

"We have some work to do. Get down here to the office." Darcy hung up before Millie could say another word. She knew that Millie would have to have a pastry and spend another thirty minutes putting on her "face" as she referred to her makeup.

An hour and a half later, Millie walked into her office with her full complement of makeup, a cup of coffee in one hand and her purse in the other. She had a habit of not knocking. If Darcy was in a meeting, her secretary would stop Millie, but if she was alone, no one stopped her.

Millie sank down into the chair. "What's up, Dee?"

They had been best friends since elementary school.

"I rushed over here, and I didn't even get my morning workout. You owe me one, girlfriend," she said as she took a small sip of coffee.

Darcy pushed the intercom button. "Monica. I know it's only been an hour, but do you have anything on Kevin Samson yet?"

Monica answered. "I have a few things. Getting his past residential history was easy. I'm still working on his past employment right now. I should have that in another hour."

"Thanks, that's a great start. Print out and bring me what you have."

"What's going on, Dee? Don't keep me in the dark. Especially when you get me up at the crack of dawn," Millie said with another yawn and sip of coffee.

Darcy shook her head at Millie's wisecrack. "Okay. Here's what's going on, as you say."

She began telling Millie what had happened yesterday, and why the police had taken Sassy in for questioning.

Millie was sitting bolt upright now. "Oh, that poor girl. She seems like such a sweet person. I can't imagine she'd kill her boyfriend."

Darcy looked at her in astonishment. "Millie! She didn't kill her boyfriend! That's why I called you here. You and I are going to prove her innocence."

"How are we going to do that?"

"By finding the actual killer. That's how!" said Darcy.

There was a knock on the office door. "Come on in, Monica," she called out.

She came in and walked over to Darcy's desk and placed a short stack of papers on it. "Good morning, Millicent," she said with a smile and a nod.

"Hey, Mon, what's up?" Millie answered.

Monica rolled her eyes at Darcy. She hated anyone calling her Mon. Millie knew she didn't like it but did it just to get a rise out of her.

"This is Kevin Samson's residence history. I have most of his employment history, and the rest should be here in maybe another hour."

"Thanks. Millie and I will leave in a few minutes. If you'll email me the rest of the employment history, I'll check it later on my tablet."

"No problem, Darcy," she said and took a quick look out of the corner of her eye at Millie.

Millicent called out to her as she left. "Nice to see you again, Mon. Have a nice day!"

Monica didn't respond as she quietly closed the door.

Millie said to Dee, "I don't think she likes me."

"You know she hates to be called Mon," said Darcy as she thumbed through the printout on her desk.

"Yeah, well, whatever. I'm out of coffee. Is there a coffee pot around here? I thought you had one in your office."

Darcy didn't look up as she answered, "Same place it always is. In the corner over there."

"Yeah, well, it's hard to see with my eyes closed in sleep this early in the morning," she said as she got up and headed for the coffeepot. She poured another cup of coffee and added cream and three spoonfuls of sugar.

"Okay, we are going to the apartment he lived in and take a look at it."

Millie frowned, cocked her head like a little puppy, and gave Darcy "the look."

"Yes, we can. We can do that. We own the building, and the management department gave him notice to move, so we have a right to enter. At least until the police arrive. They may declare it a crime scene. Then we're no longer allowed to enter until it's cleared. Do you have your camera?"

"I have my phone."

"Good enough. Let's go." Darcy got up and motioned for Millicent to follow.

"Hey, you wanna take my Lambo?" Millie asked as they entered the elevator to the garage area.

"No, we'll take my Mercedes."

"But my car attracts good-looking guys, Dee."

"I'm not looking for good-looking guys, Millie."

"I'm always looking for good-looking guys. Look at us. We are two very sexy-looking ladies. We deserve to have good-looking guys by our side," she said with a wink.

"NO! We're not taking your Lamborghini. My car is good enough."

"But it's an SUV. It's a mom car."

"True, and I'm a mom. Discussion closed."

Millicent furrowed her brows and put on a fake frown but said nothing as they walked to Darcy's SUV.

As they proceeded to the apartment complex where Kevin had lived, Millicent asked, "What are we looking for?"

"I don't know. Anything that might give us some idea of how he lived and might have prompted someone to kill him."

When they got to the complex, Darcy stopped by the rental office and got a key to the unit. She parked in front of the building, and they both went to the door and knocked.

"Why are you knocking? He's dead, isn't he?" Millicent asked.

"Yes, but he could have a friend over for a few days. We want to make sure no one is here before we enter the apartment."

"You mean like another girl?"

"Maybe, but maybe even a guy staying over for a few days. Anyone. I don't know."

"Got it, Dee." She backed away from the door just in case someone came rushing out.

No one answered, so Darcy used her key to unlock the door. As they entered, it looked like a typical "guy" apartment. There were girly magazines on the couch, and empty beer cans on the coffee table. There was a small photo album on the coffee table. Darcy picked it up, thumbed through it and dropped it into her purse. When they went into the kitchen, the sink was full of dirty dishes.

The bedroom looked typical as well. There were dirty clothes in one corner of the room, and the bedcovers were in total disarray. As they turned to leave, in another corner, they saw there was a lady's pair of panties, a bra, and two used condoms on top of the pile.

Millicent and Darcy exchanged glances.

Millicent stated, "Well, it looks like someone was having a little fun here. She left without all her belongings."

Darcy went over to the chest of drawers against the wall. She took a pair of gloves out of her purse and put them on. Then she opened the drawers one at a time.

"What are you looking for?" asked Millicent.

"Look inside the closet, Millie."

"I know. You are looking for more women's clothes, right?"

"Yes, the woman was a one-night stand. Or was she living with him? That could be why she didn't take the clothes. She had others in a drawer or the closet."

Millie nodded. "Got it!" she exclaimed. She opened the door, and hanging off to one side was a dress and a blouse.

Darcy probed through the various drawers. She found more undergarments buried under men's clothes in the bottom drawer. Someone seemed to have hidden them deliberately.

"Millie, take a picture of all these things. The clothes, the bed. Be sure to get a shot of that stain on the sheets. Touch nothing. We don't want to contaminate the scene."

"Absolutely correct, Miss Bower," said Detective Halligan as he walked into the room. "Now, leave. We are officially declaring this a crime scene."

"Hello, officer. I own this building. We gave the tenant moving notice, and we are here to check out the condition before we take possession of it again."

"After we complete our investigation, we'll clear it, and you can have it. Until then, you may not enter it." He stepped aside and gave them room to leave. Millicent continued to snap pictures as they walked out of the unit.

"One more thing, Mrs. Bower, I don't want to see you around anything that pertains to this case. Understand?" he ordered.

"Yes, we understand, officer," she answered.

"And it's detective, not officer," he called to her.

"Whatever," she said as they left.

When they got back to her car, she asked Millicent. "Did you get pictures of everything?"

"Yep, everything. I even got pictures of the good-looking cop in the living room. He didn't have a wedding ring on," she smiled. "He winked at me."

"You're incorrigible, Millie. I swear!" she laughed and started the car.

"Where to next?" Millicent asked.

"The last place he lived was in Newport News. Let's head out there."

She pulled onto Interstate Sixty-four and got off at the first exit into Newport News.

When they pulled into the apartment complex Kevin had lived in, she pulled into the visitor's place in front of the rental office. They got out and went inside. As with most rental offices, it was in one of the model units that were typical of the units in the area.

"Hello," said the woman sitting behind the desk as she looked up Darcy and Millie. "How may I help you?"

Darcy sat down in the chair in front of the desk, while Millie wandered around the apartment, checking it out.

"I'm Darcy Jean Bower, and this is my friend Millicent. We're investigating one of your previous tenants, Kevin Samson."

"Okay," she said, "but I can't give you any information on previous tenants. You understand. Privacy laws, you know."

Darcy smiled. "Of course, I understand. My family owns the Christianson Company. We have several hundred apartments in the town of Bridgeton, just a few miles closer to Richmond."

"Oh, yes. I've been to Bridgeton. Nice little town. Again, how can I help you?"

"Someone murdered Kevin Samson a couple of days ago. Millie and I are looking for reasons someone could want him dead, and maybe find his killer," stated Darcy.

"What does that have to do with us?"

"Maybe nothing, but if one of your present tenants had dealings with him, you might be harboring a killer. You wouldn't want to do that, right?"

"Isn't that the job of the police? To find killers, I mean."

"You're absolutely correct, but if someone from his past were still living here, it might tarnish the reputation of your complex. Maybe even the company that owns the complex. You don't want that now, do you?"

"Well, no. I guess not. But I might get in trouble if I give out any information."

"I can see your concern. First, Millie and I don't answer to anyone. So, the source of our information is safe with us. Next, if the police get involved, the news might cover the investigation's reach to Newport News. That would look bad for you."

The woman sat there silently, thinking. "If I tell you, I could still get in trouble if you don't have a court order."

"Not true. If the person is dead, privacy laws no longer apply."

The woman looked surprised. "Really? Privacy laws don't apply to dead people?"

"To the best of my knowledge, they don't," responded Darcy.

"Okay. I hope you're right. What did you say his name was, and when did he live here?" she asked.

Darcy gave her the dates, and she began typing. After a few moments she stopped, looked at the screen, and read the results. "Wow. Yes, I see."

"We had to give him a moving notice. He was harassing some of the single women tenants. There were several complaints about him. He moved and left the unit very dirty, so he forfeited his deposit."

"Can we have a printout of that, please, and the names of the women who registered the complaints?"

"I don't know if I can do that. There were three women. Two are gone now, but one still lives here. They aren't dead, so they have privacy."

"As I said before, we would never tell where we got the information, and if someone harassed you, wouldn't you want someone to investigate his actions? If you just give us the names of the ones who left, we can find them. We are all women here, and we need to stick together against men like that. Don't you think?"

The woman thought for a few more seconds, straightened up in her chair, and said, "Darn straight. I would want them to get what they deserved. We have our rights too, Mrs. Bower."

She printed his entire history for them. They left the office, and the resident manager felt quite pleased that she might have helped someone who was investigating a stalker. It never seemed to matter that the potential molester was now dead.

On their way out, they stopped by the one tenant who was still living there.

They got out and knocked on the door. When the woman answered, she invited them in and even offered them a beer, which they refused. She told them he didn't hurt her, but he was annoying, obnoxious, and a bit creepy but other than that he was okay. She just reported him to get him to leave her alone. The management said they would take care of it. Apparently, they did because he stopped, and a few weeks later he moved out.

By that time, it was getting late in the day. Darcy dropped Millicent off at her car, and she went home. They agreed to meet in the morning, much to Millicent's dismay that she had to get up again at the "butt crack of dawn."

That evening, Darcy ran a simple search for people finders on the internet, and the last two women showed up. One lived in Richmond. The other woman lived in Virginia Beach. The report was complete with phone numbers. Darcy talked to the woman in Virginia Beach, who had a similar story as the one she and Millie had talked to that afternoon.

She dialed the one in Richmond. Darcy introduced herself and explained the reason for her call. The lady told her a story that differed totally from the one the other woman they had talked to on the phone.

"Miss Baxter, Kevin cheated you out of over fifty thousand dollars?"

"Yes, but he was using a different name back then," she said.

"Are you sure we're talking about the same person?" asked Darcy.

"I'm sure we are. The way you describe him, it sounds like him. Do you have a picture of him?" she asked.

"Hold on." She dug into her purse and found the photo album. The same man was in many of the pictures, but all the women were different. She took one out that was a close-up photo of the man in the other pictures.

"Can I text you a picture of him?" Darcy asked as she used her phone to snap a picture of the photo.

"Yes." After a few seconds, the woman said into the phone, "That's him. That's Kevin Daniels."

"Can my friend and I stop by your home tomorrow? We'd like to talk to you and get the complete story."

"I guess so. You have my address, right?" she said.

"Yes. I have it. We'll see you at your place."

CHAPTER NINE

Darcy went to the office the next morning and got more printouts of the information Monica had gotten on Kevin Samson. She was reading the latest information she had gotten when Millie came into her office, yawning and heading straight for the coffeepot to fill her cup. She looked bleary-eyed at Darcy.

"Dee, how can you stand getting up so early each day?" she said as she yawned.

Darcy looked up at her with a grin. "It's part of being an adult, Millie," she answered.

She slid a page of the printout across her desk. "Kevin lived in four different places in six years. The last two years were at the apartment Sassy rented in her name for him. I assume he didn't pass our background checks, and that's why it was in her name instead of his."

"Yeah, yeah, yeah. Whatever," Millicent answered. "I need a cinnamon roll. Do you have any here?"

"We have some honey buns down the hall in the vending machine."

"Does the machine take credit cards?" she asked.

"No," Darcy answered without looking up from her reading. "Vending machines don't take credit cards."

"The ones at the rest stops on the interstate take cards!" she whined.

"Well, ours don't. Get some money out of my purse."

"Thanks. You're a dear, Dee."

"I know. Hurry back. I want to show you some of this stuff before we leave for Richmond to talk to Susan Baxter."

When Millicent got back in the office, she had a honey bun in one hand and a cup of coffee in the other.

Darcy looked at her. "How do you do that, Millie?"

"Do what?" she asked innocently.

"You eat junk food like a raccoon eating out of a garbage can, and you still look like a supermodel," Darcy said, looking at her with a bit of envy.

"One thing I do is I work out in my home gym for two hours each day. Which, by the way, I haven't done in two days thanks to you," she said, spinning around to show off her perfect body.

"Yeah, okay. Look at this financial report." Darcy slid the report across the table to Millie.

Millie looked down at the background report Monica had gotten on Susan Baxter.

"Look here," Darcy said, pointing at a line on Susan's financial report. "Where did she get all this money? It wasn't on the previous year's financial statement. One year later, she's got over two hundred thousand in her bank account. Where did that come from?"

Millicent sat up. Now she was awake and interested. Millie had a real knack for numbers.

She looked over the entire sheet, looking at every figure on the page. "I can't see how she made this much money on any legal investment. We need to check her out more. Something is amiss here."

Darcy laughed. "Then, let's hit the road, girlfriend."

"How did you get all this financial info?" asked Millicent as she got up.

"Monica got it. It isn't complete, just an overview. We don't have exact balances or private banking information. General information, that's all."

"I'll look deeper into Miss Baxter's financials later," said Millie.

As they passed Monica's desk, Millicent called to her, "Hey there, Monica. Great research on the Baxter girl." She gave Monica a thumbs-up as they passed.

Monica looked up, wondering why Millicent was complimenting her.

"Ha. I got her this time. She'll wonder all day why I complimented her," Millie laughed.

"You are a strange lady, Millicent Cooper," said Darcy as she punched the garage button on the elevator.

"Can we take the Lambo today?" Millie asked.

"Nope, and the discussion is closed.... again."

"Spoil sport. I look amazing today, even though it is early."

After over an hour's drive, they got to the apartment complex. Susan's apartment was on the second floor, and there was no elevator, so they took the stairs. They knocked on the door, and an attractive woman in a wheelchair opened the door and invited them inside. She was wearing stylish pants and a designer-cut blouse that looked like it had been made for her. Her shoes were simple but not the shoes one would wear around the apartment. She had flawless makeup and perfectly coiffed dark auburn hair.

They saw coffee and cookies set out as she guided them to the living room.

"How are you this morning?" she asked cordially. "Have a seat. I thought that since you might be here for a few minutes, we could talk and get to know each other. I don't get many guests, so it's a treat for me."

They sat and looked around. The apartment was tastefully decorated, with paintings on the walls and plush carpet on the floors.

Millicent spoke up. "You have very nice artwork. Do you have any originals?"

Susan responded. "Thank you. Yes, I have a couple of originals by local artists. That one over there is an original."

Millie smiled. "Is it a Claiborne? He is getting rave reviews from the critics now, and his paintings are increasing in value."

She moved her wheelchair around to see which painting Millie was pointing too, "Why, yes. It is Claiborne. You're a very astute woman. I love art."

"Have you ever been to Asheville, North Carolina?" Millicent asked.

"Yes, I have been to the art district a couple of times. I don't have any originals from an artist there, but I have a couple of limited prints. Over there," she pointed to a painting of an old barn on the far wall, "is a Number 5 of a limited print by Lionel Grant. He is an up-and-coming painter. There are only 10 editions of that one. It has already doubled in value since I acquired it. The rest are higher-number limited prints, but I liked them, so I thought I would take a chance on the artist."

"May I take a photo of them?" Millie asked as she got out her phone.

Susan hesitated and then said, "Um... sure. I guess a snapshot won't affect its value."

"Oh, no. It won't affect their value at all. I just want to show a couple of friends I saw an original Claiborne," she said as she got up and snapped a picture of the painting. She walked around and snapped some pictures of a couple of others.

Susan sat back in her wheelchair. "Now, what can I help you with? I know you didn't drive all this way to talk about my art collection."

"Before we get started on why we're here, are you an art broker?"

"No. I just dabble. I do some private sales of my own pieces, but I don't broker or sell pieces owned by others. Why do you ask? Are you interested in purchasing some art?"

Millie smiled. "I don't like to call it purchasing. I like to think of it as investing," she said, waving her arm, sweeping the air like a wand. "I buy a few pieces and trade them as others that interest me become available to me."

Susan leaned her head back and laughed. "I like your style. We're going to get along very well."

Darcy took a sip of her coffee. "We wanted to talk about Kevin. What can you tell us about him?"

"Okay, where would you like me to start?"

"How about when and where you met him?"

"We met at an art auction house. I had bid on a painting and lost the bid to another bidder." She looked over at Millicent. "Are you familiar with Houseman?"

Millicent thought for a moment. "No. I'm not. Tell me about him."

"Hahaha.... It's a woman. Emily Houseman. She is quite an up-and-coming artist. She paints mostly women in the Renaissance style. Some Madonna and old English dresses. Quite intricate."

"I see, very interesting."

"Yes. But the particular one I wanted was a bit out of my range. So, I was taking the painting I did purchase to my car when Kevin came to me and introduced himself as Kevin Daniels. From there, we kind of hit it off. If you know what I mean," she said.

"I thought when you bought a painting, they crated it and delivered it to ensure it got to its owner intact," said Millie.

"True. They do that with very expensive paintings and statue art, but what I bought wasn't that expensive, so I took it home myself."

"Yes, we understand. Excuse me for asking, but were you in a wheelchair then?"

"No. That happened about two months after Kevin and I met. Someone ran a stop sign and T-boned my car. I was in the hospital for several months, and Kevin came to see me every day, and even came to my therapy sessions. Finally, they decided they could do no more, and I'd be in a wheelchair permanently.

"Kevin insisted I sue the driver of the car. After several more months, we made a settlement. My settlement was just over half a million dollars."

"That's a nice settlement. I assume that's how you got the money to really indulge in your art investments."

"Kind of. I started investing in a few other things. Some made money, others, not so much. Are you familiar with AutoWindows?"

Millicent and Darcy shook their heads. "No," they said.

"Well, neither has anyone else. It was supposed to be the new thing. You could open your windows to let in a cool breeze. It had an alarm system option, so if anyone tried to climb in, it would alert the police, but if it rained, it would automatically close the window. It could be remotely armed and disarmed with your smartphone. You could totally control them from your phone. It could theoretically lower your cooling or heating bill at the touch of an app."

"Sounds good. What happened to it?" asked Millie.

"It was a scam. It didn't really exist. Kevin insisted it would be an excellent investment. All stores will have it by year's end. I invested one hundred thousand dollars in it. Kevin had set the whole thing up."

Darcy spoke up. "I thought you said you lost fifty thousand?"

"That was another scheme he talked me into. While we were waiting for the AutoWindows to come out, crypto was getting more popular. He told me that if we invested money in Bitcoin, we could double or triple our money in a few weeks. He even showed me printouts of the rise in the prices of Bitcoin and Ethereum. So, I bought into that as well."

"You said 'we'. Did he also put up money?" asked Millie. "He was right. Crypto skyrocketed in the past few months. You should have made a fortune."

"We opened an account in each of our names, but, like an idiot, I gave him access to my account. Once we were set up, I put fifty thousand into my account. He told me he had put an equal amount into his. That was a stupid mistake. I watched it every day as it rose. I was getting pretty excited about the money."

"Since the AutoWindow thing didn't work out, why did you invest with him again?" asked Millie.

"They were both running concurrently. We were waiting for the window thing to break into the stores. I didn't realize he was scamming me. I did some checking, and crypto is a real thing. It was all over the news. One day, Kevin was gone. So was my money. All of it. The window investment and he cleaned out my crypto account. The only true thing he said was that crypto really did triple during that time."

She took a napkin and daubed her eyes as though she was going to cry. "He took all my money. All I have left is my artwork, and I may have to sell it just to live."

"Do you know where he is now?" Darcy asked gently.

"No. I have no idea what happened to him. I assume that's why you called me. Maybe you know where he is," she said between sniffles.

"Yes. We know. He's in the Bridgeton Cemetery. He died a few days ago," said Darcy apologetically.

"Oh, no! I hoped that one day I would find him. Maybe I could have at least got the money he cheated me out of. I guess I'll never see that money again."

"If you had found him, you wouldn't have gotten anything from him. He was broke. He left nothing."

She broke down in tears. "What will I do?" she cried.

"I'm so sorry we must give you this news. We'll leave you now. If there's anything we can do, please call me." Darcy handed her one of her business cards. "We can see ourselves out."

Susan sat there, crying as they left her apartment and went back to the car.

When they got back into the car, they looked up and saw a slight movement of the curtains in one window of Susan's apartment.

"Let's go. We need to talk," said Darcy as she backed out of the parking space and moved into street traffic.

She drove until they found a coffee shop that sold breakfast croissants and pastries. Millie said that she was craving her morning sugar high.

They sat at a small table. Millie had three donuts. Darcy had a cream-cheese bagel.

"What did we find out from Susan?" Darcy asked.

Millie put down her donut and said, "She is one lying bi... woman!"

"Yep. From start to finish," answered Darcy. "First, she isn't bound to that wheelchair. There is no elevator in that building. She couldn't climb the stairs to the second floor. I also noticed slight twitches of her legs when she talked. One time, as she was telling you about her art, her right leg quivered. If she were handicapped from the waist down, I don't think they'd shake like that. I'll have to check that out. Another thing, did you see the carpet in the unit?"

Millie nodded as she took another bite of her donut.

"There were no wheelchair ruts in the carpet's pile. With regular use, it would have tire tracks in the carpet. That complex is high dollar. They all come with deep plush pile carpeting. The initial step for someone using a wheelchair would be to ask the building managers to change the carpet to hard flooring. They probably would do that, especially if she offered to pay for it. When handicapped people get what they need in a living space, they are reluctant to move. So, they make great tenants.

"Second, whatever she was into, Kevin was in it with her. They were partners. She wasn't his victim."

Another affirmative nod from Millie.

"Third, I do believe Kevin disappeared with her money. Monica could trace his background so far back. Samson is his real name, not Daniels, as she told us. I also believe she didn't know his real name, or she could have found him like we did, with a basic internet background trace."

Millie wiped her mouth and added, "If she's not really in that chair, she scammed the insurance company."

"Yes," Darcy agreed. "I bet the neighbors and the rental company don't know she is supposed to be handicapped. She said she didn't get many guests, so her chair is only for show or sympathy. We need to go back and check the parking lot. I bet she has a car there. We can run the license plates of the cars. I think I'll put a tail on her to find out what she's up to."

They finished their food, and drove back to the apartment building, and made a loop in the lot and snapped photos of all the cars and their license tags. They also noticed a security camera at each end of the parking lot.

Back at Darcy's office, Millie looked up information about the paintings in Susan's apartment. Darcy called the apartment rental company.

While Darcy was on the phone, Monica came in and placed a stack of printouts of the background search.

When Millie saw her, she gave her a thumbs up and said, "Thanks, Mon. Great work."

Monica returned a sarcastic smile as she left the room.

Darcy hung up the phone. "The resident manager is sending me copies of the parking lot surveillance video for the last two weeks. How are you doing?"

"So far, her art checks out, but I still can't find a couple of them. I'll keep working on them later. The Claiborne and the Grant seem to have been sold to her legitimately. The limited number of prints I'm having more trouble," Millie said.

"Why is it more trouble to trace the prints? They're numbered. That should make them easier to follow," said Darcy.

"Dee, Honey, prints aren't nearly as valuable and are sometimes traded privately outside of art auctions. Because of that, they are easily copied and traded. They can be basically impossible to trace. They could be legit, or fake."

"How can you tell the difference?" asked Darcy.

Millie thought for a moment. "Without X-rays and scans, you can't tell if the forgery is good enough. The sale price isn't high enough to justify the authentication cost."

Millie continued, "Let's say Susan bought one from a legitimate auction house. Then she takes the real one and has just two copies made of it. Now, she is the registered owner of the original numbered print. She quietly offers her legitimate numbered prints to two or maybe three private buyers. The cost is low enough, they see her purchase papers, and the deal is done. She does this over and over. She may not make a fortune on one, but she makes a profit on volume sales. They buy them as investments. They buy low, and hold them like you would do with a new stock IPO. Do you know what an IPO is?"

"Yes, it's an initial public offering by a new company. You buy and hope it goes up in value and price," Darcy said.

"Exactly. Local artist's work is the same way. If you don't pay a lot, even if it doesn't increase, you can usually sell it to someone who buys it because they actually like the piece. If the artist gets recognized, then the investor makes a bucketload of money," Millie said with a mock smile. "No one has them professionally authenticated, so everyone is happy."

"Does anyone ever get caught doing that?" asked Darcy.

"Very seldom. But yes, it happens, but only when an artist really hits the big time. Their work may become valuable if they die. Banksy, for example. He isn't dead yet, but his prior work was just graffiti on walls. Then one day, something happened, and he hit the big time. People are trying to steal stone walls, and there are a lot of fake Banksy walls out there."

"I never thought of it that way," said Darcy thoughtfully.

"A few years ago, there was a well-known New York auction house that was acquiring original paintings and various art objects. Instead of reselling them, they had copies made and sold the copies as originals. After a few years, their private collection of art became so big, they tried to sell the real ones. A collector realized they were offering the original of a piece of art he had bought just a few years before. The one he bought previously was a copy. The scam failed, and authentic art worth millions of dollars was released to the world. Some collectors could obtain the originals, others just lost out. It was a mess."

"I can imagine it was. What did Monica just drop in our lap?" Darcy asked as she reached for the stack of printouts.

Darcy started thumbing through the printouts. "Hey, Millie, if you'll take these pages, and sort through them, it seems that Kevin was quite the ladies' man. In the past five years, he has had a dozen or so girlfriends. Can you check through them and see if any look good as being the killer? I'll look at his work background."

As she handed Millie a stack of papers, the phone rang. She picked it up, and Mickey was on the other end of the phone.

"Dee, I just got a call from Sassy's parents. She's been picked up and charged with the murder of Kevin Samson."

Darcy took a deep breath. "Thanks, Mickey. I'll call the lawyer, and meet him at the police station." She placed the receiver in the cradle.

"Millie, they charged Sassafras with murder. You wanna come with me?"

CHAPTER TEN

s Darcy and Millie walked into the police station, they met
Patrick Donaldson, the attorney who was representing Sassy.
"Hey, Patrick. Have you talked with Sassy yet?" asked Darcy.

"Not yet. I'm trying to find her right now. I'll see if I can get an immediate hearing so a judge can set bail. Can she afford bail?" he asked.

"She's just barely making enough to pay her bills. I doubt she can afford bail."

"A murder charge will have a high bail. If she can't raise even the ten percent a bondsman will charge, she'll have to sit it out in jail until her trial. I'm sorry, Darcy, I'll do what I can, but no matter what, she will have to come up with at least the bondsman fees."

"Do what you can, Patrick."

"You know I will. To ease your mind, yes, I believe she's innocent," he added.

"Thanks, Patrick. We'll be waiting here for you."

As he walked down the hallway, Millie looked at her. "What do they have on her?"

"I don't know. Let's go talk to Detective Halligan."

When they got to his office, he hunched over a computer keyboard and cursed it. He looked up as Darcy and Millie walked in. "What do you two want?"

"We were hoping we could come to a mutual understanding," Darcy said.

"And what kind of understanding do you think we can arrive at?" he said, leaning back in his chair.

They both took seats in the office. Darcy was in front of his desk, and Millie sat in the empty chair that was beside it. Darcy was wearing a conservative blue business suit. Millie, as usual, was wearing a short mini dress. Its bright lemon-yellow color highlighted her shapely legs, which she crossed so the detective could get a good look. She leaned onto his desk and gave him a front-row seat to her ample, well-tanned bosom almost bursting out of the V-neck snow-white top she was wearing.

He ignored Millie and looked straight at Darcy. "I'm sure you want something from me. What is it you want?"

She cleared her throat. "I know that to charge Sassy with murder, you have some evidence that points to her."

"Yes, we have strong circumstantial evidence that leads directly to her."

"Can we see it?"

"No!" he said adamantly.

"How about pictures of the crime scene?" asked Millie.

"Definitely, NOT," he said emphatically.

"Why?" Millie asked.

"Because neither of you possess detective licenses, and this is an ongoing investigation..."

"An ongoing investigation. I know that routine." Darcy interrupted his answer.

"So, you understand how this works. Good day, ladies. Now I need to fill out some paperwork, if you will excuse me. I have to fill out my DD5 reports."

Millie stood up and leaned over his keyboard and typed a few words. "There you go, Detective Halligan. There is your DD5 form. Just fill in the blanks."

He looked up at her, thought for a moment, and said, "Okay, I'll give you this, but it didn't come from me. Understand?"

"Of course, Detective," smiled Millie as she sat back down.

"We have the stone he was struck on the back of his head with...."

"That's all you've got? That proves nothing," said Darcy.

"True, but the bench where they were sitting has Sassy's fingerprints on it. That proves she was there at the scene," he added.

"And so are a thousand other people. It's a public bench, Detective!" added Millie.

He never took his eyes off Darcy. "Mrs. Bower. Also, true. We found many other prints that we're checking out, but hers were fairly fresh, as well as a couple of others."

"Who are the other prints matched with?" asked Darcy.

"We don't have any matches yet, but we'll keep looking. Even if we find other matches, Miss Magill is the only one that has the MMO. That stands for..."

Millie shifted in her seat, noting he refused to look at her, and interrupted him. "We know what it stands for, Detective. Motive, means, and opportunity."

Continuing eye contact with Darcy, he continued, "Even if we get a match on some other people's prints on that bench, we can't investigate every person in Bridgeton for a motive."

"Instead, you would rather put an innocent victim of fraud and deceit in jail for the rest of her life, just to keep up your conviction rate stats, detective! You make me sick!" Millicent rose from her chair and headed for the door.

Halligan watched in silence as both women walked out of his door.

As they walked down the hall, Millie stated. "I think he's gay, as well as a jackass."

Darcy turned and looked at her. "What makes you think that?"

"Did you see the way he looked at me?" Millie said.

"He didn't look at you at all. That is until you almost dumped your... things... on his desk."

"That's what I'm talking about. What straight man could resist this?" she said, waving her hands up and down her body.

"That doesn't make him gay?"

"It does to me," Millie said. "And, also a jackass."

"Oh, my goodness. Let's get out of here before you embarrass me to death," Darcy stated sarcastically.

CHAPTER ELEVEN

Even though it was late in the day, Millie insisted she had to get her daily gym workout, so she headed for home. Darcy went back to her office. She wanted to get a copy of the police files on the investigation.

She looked at the pages of printouts of the jobs Kevin had held over the years. The last one he had was with a law firm right in Bridgeton. The firm of Lawrence and Riggles. She looked up the phone number and called it.

"Lawrence and Riggles law offices, how may I help you?" said the voice at the other end of the line.

"Hello, this is Darcy Jean Bower. I'm doing some background work on Kevin Samson. I understand he used to work for your firm."

"I'm sorry, but I have only been here for a few months, so I know nothing about that, ma'am," the girl said.

"Is there someone I can talk to about it?"

"I can transfer you to Mr. Riggles. Hold on, please."

After a few moments, a man with a very gruff voice picked up the line. "How can I help you?"

"I'm Darcy Jean Bower. I'm doing some background checks on Kevin Samson."

"Okay. What about him?"

"Can you tell me why he left your firm?"

"That's personal information. I don't give out that information."

"Did he leave on good terms, sir?"

"What part of I don't give out that information, do you not understand?"

"All I need to know is, did he leave on good terms?"

"No, do not call here again!"

"Would you give him a good recommendation, sir?"

"No. This conversation is over. Do not call here again," he said, and the line went dead.

"Well, thank you, sir," she said to a dead line.

Apparently, Kevin wasn't well-liked there either. She and Millie would need to look deeper into that as well.

She dialed the phone again, and the same girl answered. "Lawrence and Riggles law offices, how may I help you?"

"Hi, there. I called you a few minutes ago. Can you give me the name of the receptionist who worked there before you?"

"Oh, yes, ma'am. She worked here for a long time. Hold on. I'll get it for you."

In a few seconds, the girl was back. "The last person was Tracy Larson. She was here forever."

"Thank you. May I ask why she left?"

"She got pregnant and went out on maternity leave. When she left, they hired me to replace her."

"Do you know why she didn't come back after the baby was born?"

"Well, I was supposed to be here temporarily until then, but she just never came back. I don't know why."

"Thank you. Have a nice day," Darcy said.

"You too, ma'am," she answered.

Darcy ran a check and got her present phone number and dialed it. When a woman answered the phone, Darcy asked. "Is this Tracy Larson?"

"Yes, it is. Who is this?" she answered.

"I'm Darcy Jean Bower. If you have a few minutes, I'd like to ask you a few questions about Kevin Samson."

"What did that SOB do now? I hope he rots in hell!" Tracy said.

"Okay, that answers some of my questions. First, both of you worked for Lawrence and Riggles. Correct?"

"Yes."

"Can a friend and I stop by and talk with you about him?"

"Yes, but give me a couple of hours. I have some shopping to do for the baby."

"Thanks, it's getting late. If you don't mind, we'll stop by first thing in the morning. Say about 9 AM?"

"Sure. That's fine," Tracy said.

Darcy called Millie and told her about their appointment with Tracy. Darcy said she would stop by Millie's house and pick her up. The following morning, when Darcy got there, she parked and walked into Millie's house without knocking. As she walked in, she saw Millie standing in the entrance hallway in front of a full-length mirror smoothing her clothes.

"You don't knock anymore, Dee?"

"Do I need too? You barge into my office all the time without knocking," Darcy said sarcastically. "You look good, by the way."

"I know it. I worked out for a full two hours at my gym. I'm ready for the world. Let's go. And we are taking the Lambo this time."

"No."

"Yes. I insist," Millie said.

"Okay, but please don't drive so rough. You don't even know how to drive smoothly," Darcy warned.

"When you drive a Lamborghini, you're required to step on it sometimes," she said, walking out the door.

When Darcy came out and closed the door, Millie pointed a remote, and the front door gave a click. Millie strutted out and again aimed another remote at the car, and the doors clicked to unlock. They got in and buckled up. Millie backed out slowly but gunned it when they got into the street.

"Hey, slow down. It's a car, not a roller coaster," she called to Millie.

"You're required to drive one like this. Don't you ever watch old Magnum P.I. shows?"

"He drives a Ferrari," said Darcy.

"Same principle," she said, but let off the speed a bit. "Where are we going?"

Darcy gave her an address, and Millie looked at her and said, "Hold on, you're in for a bumpy ride."

"Who said that anyway? It's an old saying. Some movie star said it. Who was that?" asked Darcy.

Millie responded, "It was Bette Davis in the 1950 movie All About Eve. The correct line was, and I quote 'Fasten your seatbelts, it's going to be a bumpy night.'"

Darcy leaned her head back against the headrest. "You and my father are the only people I know who would know that? That movie was released before we were born. It was made before my father was born! It's beyond antique!"

Millie smiled. "Yeah. But some of those old movies were really awesome. I love them."

"Yeah. I know you do. You stay up half the night watching them."

"I think you're jealous. That's all." She reached over and turned the radio on to 1960s music, and they listened as Millie drove. A few minutes later, they pulled into a small house on a cul-de-sac.

As they got to the door, it opened, and a lady in her early thirties was holding a baby on her hip. She was wearing hip-hugger jeans that went out of style years ago, but had the in-style rips in the knees. She was cute, but had a sad look about her, as many lower-income family mothers seemed to have. They could tell at one time she had the same hope as many young girls, but lost it in marriage and motherhood. Her dreams crushed, now takes life just one day at a time.

"I heard you drive up. Wow, that is some fancy car!" she said. "Come on into the house."

"Thank you, I'm sure everyone on the block heard us drive up," said Darcy as she gave Millie "the look."

She led them to the back of the small house, where the living room was located, and put the baby in a playpen. "Can I offer you anything to drink? I mean a soda or water. That's all I have unless you would like a glass of milk."

"No, thank you," said Darcy.

"Yes, thanks but no for me too," added Millie.

They each sat at opposite ends of a small couch, and Tracy sat in a small upholstered chair that matched the fabric on the couch.

"What can I tell you about Kevin?"

"Why don't you start at the beginning?" said Millie.

"Umm. Let's see, I started at Lawrence and Riggles as a part-time researcher. Kevin came on a couple of months later because they had a couple of large cases. We worked together."

"I didn't think Bridgeton was large enough to have big cases. Christianson Company is the biggest company in the town," said Millicent matter-of-factly.

"It is, but with the internet, most things are online now. Even the law library is online. Forty years ago, you literally had to go down and use a card catalogue and pull books from a shelf to look something up. Now you sit at a desk, type, and research items. When you find what you're looking for, you copy and paste, and then you can email most things. However, they will digitize the system in a few years, such as in some large cities like New York."

"After a few months, we moved in together. All went well. Then Mrs. Riggles got pregnant, and it hit the fan. I didn't know it at the time, but Kevin was the father."

"He told her he had a vasectomy, but he didn't. He was sleeping with both of us. AT THE SAME TIME!" she said.

"I wasn't using any birth control either. The doctor said I had an angry vagina."

Darcy and Millie looked at each other with a definite question here.

"What's an angry vagina? Is that a real thing?" Darcy asked.

"Yes. It is a real thing. It's kind of complicated to describe, so I'll let you look it up later. Basically, it makes it extremely difficult for me to get pregnant, so I wasn't worried. Kevin also told me he had a vasectomy."

"This sounds crazy, but I've heard that men like married women because they can blame the woman's husband if she gets pregnant," said Darcy.

"I've heard that too, but in this case, I was a widow, and Mr. Riggles really had a vasectomy. So, she was sleeping with a man who lied about his vasectomy, and her husband, who had a real one."

"Mrs. Riggles got an abortion, but because of some mistake at the abortion clinic, Mr. R found out about it. She admitted the affair with Kevin, and Mr. R fired him. We were still sleeping together, and I found out the next month that I was pregnant too."

"So even with your angry... thing, you got pregnant?" Millie said, waving her hand in front of her pants.

"Yep. He tried to get me to have an abortion, but I refused. I said he should help support my baby."

"What happened?" asked Darcy.

"He walked out on me."

"Were you living together then?" asked Millie.

"Not really. He would spend some nights with me, and some nights at his place, but when I told him I was pregnant, he stopped coming over and just cut me off.

"After I left the law office, I got a job as a receptionist at the local hospital so that I could continue my insurance coverage until I had the baby. Then I quit."

"Are you working now?" continued Millie.

"I don't really need to. I was married before I met Kevin, but my husband died a few years ago from cancer. We had insurance for everything. The house mortgage, the car loan, and he had a life insurance policy. His family on his father's side all died young. He knew his chances of dying of cancer were high, so he insured everything he could. Now I wish my child was his, not that a-hole Kevin."

"Have you seen him lately?" asked Darcy.

"I haven't seen him for over a year. I hope I never see him again. He was always trying to work some side game."

"What do you mean by side game?"

"He was always trying to get someone to invest in some new business and even trying to get people to trade crypto. I don't really know. He was a hustler. A con man."

"Do you have any names of people who invested money with him?"

"I remember he mentioned two people. Keven tried to get them to invest in some kind of window replacement. Another thing he wanted them to buy was some cryptocurrency. That's getting really big now, you know."

"Yes, we know. What was the name of the window company?"

I don't know. SmartWindow, or something like that, I think."

"You mean, AutoWindow?"

"Yes, that was it! He got someone to invest over a hundred thousand dollars in it."

"Which cryptocurrency was he promoting?" asked Millicent.

"That's easy. It was a new cryptocurrency startup called Greencoin. Only companies that produced green, earth-friendly products backed it."

"Physical companies do not back or produce cryptocurrencies, Tracy," added Millicent.

"Yeah. I know that now, but I didn't know it when Kevin and I were together."

"Did you invest any money in his scheme?" continued Millicent.

"Only a few thousand dollars. I had very little money to give him. He promised me I'd be rich in just a few years, when the green companies took off. That was all a lie. There were no green companies backing the crypto. Yes, I lost my money, but it wasn't like some other people he scammed."

"Did you meet any of the other investors?"

"Yes. I met two of them. We went to dinner with an investor named Satchel Hollis. We had a business lunch with Gary Grayson. But that's all," Tracy said.

"Did you see them give Kevin any money?"

"At dinner, Mr. Hollis gave Kevin a check for one hundred fifty thousand dollars. Mr. Grayson wasn't rich, and all he could afford was ten thousand. He had a wife and two kids. Kevin promised him huge profits when things gained momentum."

"What were they investing in?"

"That window company. But when it went bankrupt, everyone lost their money," she said sadly. "Mr. Hollis was doing okay financially. Gary was a nice guy. He was an ordinary guy. A welder at the Newport News Shipyard. I'm sure it hit him hard, but Kevin didn't care. His answer to that was, all investments have a certain risk, and they knew that going in. He said it wasn't his fault. 'Win some, lose some' was his response."

"He was one cold guy, wasn't he?" Millicent commented sadly.

"Yes. He was."

"You won't hear from him again," Darcy said. "Someone killed him a few days ago."

"I can't say I'm sorry. I'm not glad. Just not sorry, that's all."

"Can you give us any information about Mrs. Riggles? We'd like to talk with her as well."

"After the affair, Mr. R divorced her. She committed suicide."

"How did she do it?" asked Darcy.

"I don't remember. Initially, the police said someone had murdered her, but then they changed their statement to suicide. I don't remember all the details."

"One last thing. You said you didn't need to work because your husband left you some money. So why were you working?" questioned Darcy.

"Well, even though everything is paid for, I can live, but the insurance money won't last forever. Every bit I earn will make what I have in the bank last longer," she said matter-of-factly.

"You're a smart lady, Tracy. If you decide to go back to work, call us. We're always looking for sharp people," Darcy added as she handed her a card. "Thank you for your time."

As Millie pulled back onto the street, she asked Darcy, "What do you think of her?"

Darcy thought for a few moments. "I don't know. She sounds legitimate. We need to delve more into her finances and Mrs. Riggles' suicide."

"I agree. Let's just take the day off, and ride around." Millie laughed as she shifted into high gear.

"You can't take a day off. You don't have a job. Every day is a day off for you!" Darcy said as she laid her head against the headrest. She knew Millicent was going to punch the accelerator and snap her head against it anyway. Millicent loved fast cars as much as any guy she knew.

Millicent went up the interstate on-ramp and continued to speed up. As the engine wound up, the wind blew over the windshield and made a tremendous whooshing sound. When Darcy looked over at the speedometer, she saw it creeping past one hundred and ten.

She tapped Millicent on the arm, and called to her, "Hey, take it back down. You'll either get us killed or put in jail when we get pulled over by the state police!"

Millicent gave her a fake sad face and let the car slow down. "Spoil sport!"

"I want to sleep in my own bed tonight, not a jail cell or a hospital bed."

Soon they were back at Millicent's home and sitting in her den looking at more printouts that Monica had given them on Kevin.

The den area is where Millie spent most of her time, just as many people do. It was her entertainment room and her makeshift office when she didn't want to sit in her home office. It had a sectional couch with a large glass-topped coffee table, and an ottoman at each end. Mounted on the main wall across from the couch was a huge flat-screen television.

Below the television were two large speakers that could shatter glass if turned up to full volume. In another corner was an office-quality wireless printer, similar to the one in her home office. There were various potted plants, some real, others excellent fake ones. Also, various paintings adorned the walls. Millie loved art, but the art reflected her way of life, disorganized and abstract. She was a living version of the Hollywood version of "Thoroughly Modern Millie." She was wild and free, and her home reflected her zany personality.

"Millie, can you look up Mrs. Riggles and see what was reported about her suicide?"

"Honey, I can look up her last gynecologist lab report."

"I don't need that," Darcy called back to her.

"Yeah, while you're in there, look in the upper cupboard over the coffeepot. Get the bottle of Irish whiskey. And pour a shot, would you do that?"

"Okay, but it's early afternoon. It's a bit early to be drinking, isn't it, Millie?" called Darcy from the kitchen.

"It's never too early for a shot of Irish whiskey," Millicent answered.

"Touche'," Darcy answered. She looked out the window of Millicent's kitchen. Millie had a kidney-shaped swimming pool surrounded by lounge chairs, metal tables and matching chairs. Darcy remembered when Millie and her husband used to host parties with friends from all over town. Since Millie had divorced, Darcy remembered no more parties.

She took two cups from the cabinet, and a bottle of whiskey. She poured a shot into each of the two cups. When she headed back to the den area, she heard Millicent on the phone. "Okay. Thanks, Will. I owe you one." She hung up the phone. "Dee. Willard White will email us the complete investigation file on Mrs. Riggles' death. It'll be here within the hour. Let's go sit by the pool."

Darcy handed her a cup as Millicent stood and headed to the door leading to the pool. As they got outside, they saw the pool boy unloading a hose and some cleaning supplies and equipment.

He looked up, and then nodded. "Would you like me to come back later, so I won't be in your way, Mrs. Cooper?" he called to Millicent.

"No. We'll only be here for a couple of minutes, Darren," she answered.

She looked over at Darcy and winked. "Kind of a hunk, isn't he?"

"Is it true about handsome pool boys?" Darcy laughed.

"No, he's just the pool boy. Nothing more, Dee! Besides, he's way too young for me!"

They sat and watched the well-tanned, muscled young man do his job until Millicent's phone buzzed. She picked it up and looked at the text on the screen. "I think the email we're waiting for has arrived."

Back in her home office, Millicent opened the email and started printing the entire police file on Janet Riggles. When the printer stopped, they took the paper back to the den, sat down and started reading.

Darcy looked at the autopsy report and passed it to Millicent. "Look at this. The place Janet Riggles was found in was the apartment she had rented after the divorce. Her system had high levels of alcohol and phenobarbital. Her eyes showed signs of retinal hemorrhage, and her hyoid bone was severely bruised. Someone killed Janet. It was not suicide!"

"How did you decide that? The coroner said it was suicide!"

"Take it one step at a time. First, she was drugged with phenobarbital, probably some pills ground up and mixed with the alcohol, making her easy to manage. She was basically high. The killer could have forced her to drink the alcohol. To speed up her death, he gently strangled her. Not with enough force to break the hyoid bone in her neck, but just enough to restrict her breathing and cause the retinal hemorrhage," explained Darcy.

Millicent nodded in agreement. "I can see that. Why would the coroner say that if it wasn't true?"

"I don't know. Let's ask him," Darcy suggested. Just then, her phone buzzed. She answered it. "Hello, Mickey Ray."

"Hey, Dee. The lawyer got an emergency hearing with the judge. They set bail at three hundred thousand dollars. A bondsman will want ten percent to bail her out."

"Yeah, bond fees are usually ten percent. That's thirty thousand dollars. Sassy doesn't have that kind of money. What do you want to do?"

"I don't know. She's not a flight risk, but even when she shows up in court, the bondsman keeps the thirty grand. I like her, but should we put up that kind of money?"

"We can't just let her sit in jail," added Darcy.

"I'll call the bank. Maybe she can put up the store as collateral for the bond fees?" Mickey suggested.

"Yes, but even doing that, when we clear her name, she'll owe that money back to the bank and the total losses she incurred to Kevin."

"I know, and it sucks, but life isn't always fair, Dee. At least she'll be free. Not in jail on a murder charge."

"Okay. See what you can do. I'll work on things from my end," she clicked off and told Millicent what Mickey said.

"Wow, win or lose, she still loses," Millicent said.

"Yep. Sometimes life sucks. Now let's get in touch with the coroner."

Darcy called the local hospital, where all the autopsies were done in Bridgeton for the police department. They informed her that Dr. Wilson had retired. And even verified his date of retirement.

Mickey called her and informed her that Mr. Compton from the bank would go to the county jail with documents for Sassy to sign. He would arrange for a bank loan, putting her store up for collateral to pay for her release from custody. That way, they didn't have to pay a bail bondsman. Mickey would also agree to co-sign the loan.

Darcy didn't like the idea of Mickey signing the loan. "Mickey, if something happens, we're on the hook for three hundred thousand dollars. I don't like that one bit," she said.

"No, dear sister. I'll be on the hook for it. Besides, if that happens, we'll foreclose on the store. Nothing will happen. I have faith in her."

"You are much more naïve than I, Mickey Ray Christianson. I wouldn't put my name on anyone's loan for bail money."

Millicent had her head buried in her own world, looking up things online. She knew her way around the internet.

"What are you looking for now, Millie?" Darcy asked.

"We need the bank statements for Doctor Blanton Wilson. He was the city coroner for thirty years and retired a few years ago," she said.

"Why do you need those? And how far back do you need them?" asked Darcy.

"Remember the cop rule in investigations? Follow the money!" she said, answering her own question. "It's obvious that someone killed her. We saw that on the autopsy report. If we saw it, then someone else saw it too, but buried it. Also, we need to find out who the district attorney was at that time."

"Why do we need to investigate the district attorney?"

"The DA determines whether there is enough evidence to move forward and present evidence to a grand jury. If the medical examiner says it was suicide, then the DA will drop the case and close it."

"You're scary. You know way too much about police and legal procedures," added Darcy.

"I've got to go into the deep web to get this info. It'll take me a while," said Millicent as she typed.

"What's the deep web?"

"Simply put, there's the surface web. That's what the public pulls up when they go online. The deep web is where private information is stored. Banks use it to keep all your banking information. Medical facilities use it to store medical records, and all that HEPA stuff. The government keeps all of its information, including all the military records. Finally, there is the dark web. It's where the dregs of society go to do their illegal business. Criminals go there to make business deals. High-level drug dealers, arms dealers, all that really nasty stuff goes on in the dark web. The government constantly monitors it. Without a VPN, a government agency could show up, raid your place, and seize your computer. Then you'll spend a lot of time in jail waiting for a complete investigation of your entire life. And the government will monitor you for the rest of your life."

Darcy furrowed her brow at this information. "What's a VPN?"

Millicent took a deep breath and explained, "A virtual private network is a computer program that you load on your computer. It's the only defense against someone backtracking and tracing your location. I'm serious. You do not want to mess around on the dark web without one."

"Do you have that program loaded on your computer?" asked Darcy.

Millicent just looked at Dee, then returned to her keyboard. Darcy knew not to press her for any further information about that subject.

"While you're at it, why don't you get some financial records on Susan Baxter?"

"Will do," Millicent answered. She had to have money to get started with her art collection.

CHAPTER TWELVE

Mr. Compton had all the papers for Sassafras to sign, and Mickey signed as a co-signer of the loan. As the banker got up, he handed the paperwork to the attorney to file with the county court and provided the necessary paperwork so Sassy could go home.

Sassy reached out to Mickey and gave him a big hug, and with tears in her eyes, she thanked Mickey.

"Okay, you understand that you can't leave town, and of course you must show up in court on the date specified in the document. Right?" Mickey said.

"Yes, Mickey. I understand. I'll be thankful to you for the rest of my life for helping me out."

"If you leave the city limits, I will lose my money, and I will take the store to recover it. You understand?"

She nodded her head between sniffles.

"Good. Now let's get you home and get that store up and running again," Mickey said as he led her out of the room.

As they pulled up to the front of the store, Reilly and Jaime were there waiting for her. They stood up and clapped. Jaime gave her a big hug, and Reilly shook her hand. She understood his aversion to being touched.

People in the town heard that she had been arrested for Kevin's murder, and when she opened the store, customers again crowded inside. In a few days, as the last time, her shelves were bare, and she placed another large order.

When Glenda answered, she said, "Sassy, I keep hearing about all the things happening. I hope you're alright."

"Yeah, Glenda, the people of Bridgeton have been wonderful and very supportive of me."

"I'm so glad to hear that. What can I send to you today?"

"Well, first, you can send that nice delivery man, Josh. Did he tell you he even stayed and helped to put the stock on our shelves?"

Glenda laughed. "No. He didn't tell me that. Our drivers rarely do that. He said, y'all were very nice, and he enjoyed helping all of you. He said every time he said something nice to Jaime she would blush."

"Jaime likes the attention. People don't see us as regular people, and they don't know how to respond to us. I have cerebral palsy, Jaime has Down syndrome, and Reilly is autistic. People come in and are surrounded by people who are different. I walk funny and even talk a bit slurred, but I'm a person. People don't talk to Jaime because they don't know if she understands what they are saying. She understands, and she knows when people are nice and if she is being shunned. She has feelings just like all of us. And it makes her feel good when someone just greets her. When they complement her, it really makes her day. Reilly is a different person with unique problems. He's in his own world. He doesn't care if nobody speaks to him, but if they do, he responds in kind. If you ask him if it's a nice day, he may not know how to answer. If you tell him, it's a nice day, he will probably agree with you, no matter what the day is like."

"I'm sure that the work environment at your store is very nice," added Glenda.

"Usually, it is. If someone comes in a foul mood, Jaime can tell. Reilly will ignore a customer if they don't approach him, but Jaime picks up on moods quickly. If they are rude to her, she gets upset, and I have to calm her down. But all in all, things are good here."

Glenda said, "Okay, I have just received your email order. Can you make it through the day?"

"Yes, we're totally out of a few things, but mostly, we can hold out a day, maybe two."

"Great. I'll have them load your order in the truck last, so that your order will come off the truck first. That way, Josh will be at your store early for the day's sales. Maybe he'll help you with things again."

"I don't expect him to do that. I know it's not his job," Sassy said.

"True, it isn't, and I can't tell him to do it, but maybe he will do it just as he did last time. My other line is ringing. Gotta go, Sas. Have a great day!" Glenda said and hung up.

Sassy was happy, and she told Jaime and Reilly about the order, which would be delivered early the next day.

Reilly just looked at her. "You and Jaime like Josh, the driver, don't you?"

Jaime clapped her hands like a little child who had received a present. "Yeah, Reilly. He's nice and so pretty!"

Sassy laughed. "That's handsome. Girls are pretty. Men are handsome, Jaime."

"Yeah. That's what I meant. He's handsome," giggled Jaime.

For all three of them, the day dragged on, but customers were still flooding in to support her, so it wasn't boring. They kept busy the rest of the day.

Customers flooded in and bought minor items. Sassy knew they didn't need to show their love and support. One person came in and got a six-pack of soda. Another got a couple of rolls of toilet paper and a package of paper towels. One lady came in with her two children and bought them each a bar of candy and a soda. Most refused their change, saying they didn't like the coins jingling in their pocket or purse. She knew it was a subtle way of giving her additional support. Reilly wasn't pleased with it. It threw his bookkeeping off. The cash register amount didn't match up with the computer printout.

After they closed, Sassy took the extra money out of the register tray and divided it between Jaime and Reilly. Jaime was pleased. Reilly had a hard time understanding why Sassy had done that. She had to insist, but he accepted the money.

Shortly after opening the following morning, they saw the delivery truck pull to the side door of the store, and Jaime put on her biggest smile. Reilly just stood with a blank expression. He didn't understand the excitement. To him, it was just another delivery.

Since it was a side door used mainly for supply delivery, he didn't knock. He just opened the door and pushed a loaded hand truck through it. "Hey," he called out. "Anyone home?"

Jaime almost ran to the back door and greeted him. "Hi, Josh!" she said to him.

"Hello, Jaime. How are you today?"

She lowered her head like a shy schoolgirl. "I'm fine."

"I've got another big delivery for you again. Would you like me to help you put it on the shelves, like I did the last time?"

Jaime gave him a big smile as she nodded her head yes.

As the last customer left, Sassy went back to the stockroom, where Jaime and Reilly were helping Josh bring the boxes inside. When they had brought them in, Josh moved the boxes into the store area. They all put items on the shelves, and Jaime put them in their proper order.

It took nearly an hour to re-stock the shelves, and then they all sat down on the floor. Josh got up and took drinks out of the cooler and gave one to Jaime, Reilly, and Sassy. He opened the last one for himself. He dropped several dollar bills on the counter beside the register.

"And what are you doing?" asked Sassy.

"Paying for the drinks I bought," he answered as he sat down on the floor. The others followed suit. In a few seconds, they were all sitting on the floor, almost in a circle.

"Are you kidding me? After all you did to help us out?" she asked.

"Yep," he said as he took a big swig of his drink.

"I pay my employees, and you don't buy me a drink from my own store. Last, I should be paying you, and I owe you a lot more that a cold soda pop."

He laughed and put the bottle on the floor beside him. "I don't see your point, little lady."

"Little lady?" she questioned. "I mean…" she started to say when he interrupted her.

"I know what you mean, but I want to do it. I pay my own way. You own me nothing but a date," he said sheepishly. "And as far as the term, little lady. I'm from Texas. We say that all the time."

Sassy ignored his explanation of "little lady" and asked, "What kind of date?"

"A regular date. You know, dinner and maybe a movie. That's all."

"I don't know you well enough to date you, Josh," she said, followed by a sip from her bottle.

"Isn't that the reason for a date? To get to know each other, I mean?"

"Yeah. I guess it is," she replied. "I don't even know your last name."

"Okay. My name is Josh Turner. Is that good enough?" he grinned again.

"No. Not really," she said. "I thought I knew the man I had hoped to marry, but he turned out to be a cheat."

"Okay. I get it. But I'm allowed an hour for lunch every day. What if we meet for lunch at the Burger Shack down the street tomorrow, and I'll buy your lunch? We can get to know each other during that hour," he suggested.

"I guess I could do that, but we go Dutch," she said.

"I've never heard that term before. What does that mean?" he asked.

"It means we each pay our own tab."

"No, definitely not. I don't ask a girl out and expect her to pay her way." He drank the last few sips in the bottle, then got up, and put it in the bottle rack.

"I have a few rules of my own, Josh Turner. On the first date, I pay my own way. If we decide we want another one, then you can pay."

"I pay, or it's no deal," he said adamantly. "In Texas, we believe in treating a lady with respect."

"You're not in Texas, Josh Turner. You are in Virginia, in the town of Bridgeton, and in my store. These are my rules from now on. I guess we don't have a deal."

"Why?" he asked.

"I have my reasons, and at this point, I don't have to give you a reason for my decisions."

He just stood there, looking down at her still sitting on the floor. "I like you, Sas. I was hoping we could be friends, but I think you have made it clear you are not interested in my company outside of being your delivery man. I have to get back and turn in the truck. Good morning, Miss Magill." He walked out the door and closed it gently.

Reilly sat saying nothing.

Jaime looked at Sassy in the sad way only she could do. "Why did you do that, Sassy? Don't you like him? He's nice to me." She got up, got her purse from under the counter. As Jaime walked toward the door. "Can I go home early, please?"

"Wait, Jaime. He didn't mean it. Really. I agree, he's a very nice man," called Sassy. She got up and tried to follow Jaime but couldn't keep up with her. Jaime softly closed the door and disappeared.

Reilly got up and followed Jaime. As he reached the door, he turned to her. "Do you want me to lock the door when I get outside?"

"No. I don't want you to leave me here. I need some help today, Reilly. I need you," Sassafras called to him.

"Okay." He turned around and went back to the register.

Walking dejectedly back to the stockroom, she sat down on a pallet of automotive accessories. She looked up and stared at the ceiling. She prayed. "What's wrong with me, God? Why am I this way? Josh is such a nice person. He didn't deserve my reaction to his kindness. Show me what I'm supposed to do." She leaned back against the shelves, closed her eyes. And quietly cried. She laid her head down on the low pallet next to the one she was sitting on and fell asleep.

Someone was gently touching Sassy's shoulder. She raised her head, and it was Jaime, also with tears in her eyes. "I'm sorry, Sassy. I didn't mean to make you cry. I won't do it again. I was sad because you had made Josh angry."

She reached up and pulled Jaime down beside her and held her close against her. "My dear sweet Jaime. You did nothing wrong. It was me. I was stupid. I made a big mistake, and you have every right to be angry with me. Don't cry, Jaime."

"But I hurt you. You are my favorite person in the world," Jame said.

"You didn't hurt me. I hurt myself sometimes because I don't know what to do. You are one of the best people in my world too."

They sat in each other's grasp, seeking comfort from each other. After a few minutes, Sassy stroked Jaime's hair as a mother would do for her child. "Let's just go back to work and forget this whole thing happened. Let's make it a great day."

"Okay. I'll just pretend it's a good day. I'll do it for you, Sassy." Jaime pulled away and looked into Sassy's eyes with the innocence of a little girl.

They got up and went back into the front room and went to work. At the end of another good day of sales, Sassy went into the back room and pulled herself up the stairs and dropped onto her bed.

The store phone awakened her, ringing. She had an extension in her bedroom, so she reached across the bed to answer it.

"Sassafras Magill. What in the world did you say to Josh!" said Glenda.

"What do you mean?" Sassy said sleepily into the phone.

"I was still here last night doing some scheduling for today's deliveries when Josh came in. I could tell he was angry. He said hardly a word. He just said he wanted a different route in the future," said Glenda.

"We kind of had words. I didn't mean for it to turn out badly."

"What happened, Sassy?"

"I'd rather not talk about it."

"Girl, I've known you since you were born, now tell me!" Glenda insisted.

"Seriously, Glenda. I just don't want to talk about it."

"Okay, I'll assign Josh to another route for a few weeks. Just get your act together. He's a really nice guy."

"I know he is. That's the problem. I'm not. I'm broken, Glenda."

"No. You are not broken, but you need to get your head straight. I won't push you right now, but you need to do some soul searching, girl. Give me a call when you're ready. I'm here for you."

"Thanks, you're a good friend," she said and hung up the phone. When she looked at the clock on her bedside, she knew she had to get up and open the store. It was going to be a very stressful day. Chronic pain was one of the side effects of her spastic cerebral palsy. She frequently ached when she got up in the mornings and needed to exercise to loosen up her muscles.

When she went downstairs, Jaime and Reilly were already getting the store ready to open. Reilly had booted up the store's main computer. Jaime was dusting shelves and placing the stock in its proper place, just as she did many times each day.

"Good morning, Sassy," both Jaime and Reilly chimed in at the same time. They each giggled at their morning greetings to her.

"Good morning to both of you too," Sassy answered. "I hope we all have a great day."

"We hope we have a good day too," Jaime answered. "How was your night?"

"It was good," Sassy lied. She had a horrible night. But she didn't want to upset them. Especially Jaime.

She tried to be busy herself, so her mood wouldn't affect them. As much as she tried, Jaime knew her mood, but left her alone.

They kept busy with customers all morning, and when Reilly got back from his lunch break, she told Jaime to take hers. Jaime came up to her and put her arms around Sassy. "I'm sorry you are sad. I love you, and I want you to be happy, not sad."

Sassy hugged Jaime. "I know. You are such a sweet young lady. I love you, too. I will be happy again. It'll just take me a few days. Don't worry about me." She gently pushed Jaime away, looked at her and smiled. Jaime returned her smile.

They had a steady flow of customers all day, and things went smoothly. She noticed that her car was gone. When she made some calls, she found out it was in the police impound so the Crime Scene Investigation team could go over it.

CHAPTER THIRTEEN

Millie typed away while Darcy pored over the printouts Monica had gotten for her. She had asked Monica to dig up everything she could find about Kevin Samson. Monica couldn't get his banking information, and Darcy felt she needed that information as well.

Millicent looked up and said, "I can get this information, but it isn't as easy as they portray on television and in the movies."

"How long will it take?" Darcy asked.

"It could take me an hour, or all day. I have a program that I use, but there are thousands of combinations of passwords, and some sites are encrypted to keep people like us out of it."

"Okay, while you're doing that, I have some work I need to do at the office. Call me when you get the info," Darcy said as she got up and headed toward the front door.

"Got it," Millicent said without even looking up from her computer.

Darcy worked on the monthly reports of the construction company she and her brother owned while waiting for Millicent to work her magic on the computer. Mickey poked his head around the corner of her office door. "Knock, knock," he called to her.

Looking up, she said, "Come on in, Mickey Ray. How's your day going so far?"

"I guess it's going okay," he said as he took a seat in front of her desk. "How is your investigation going?"

"Millie is digging for more information. The more we find out, the more information we need. The whole thing seems like cancer, and the more we expose, the worse it looks."

"In what way, Dee?"

Darcy put down her pen and leaned back in her chair. "Kevin Samson was thoroughly a bad person. Millie and I are still looking at his past, but the more we dig up, the more cancer we see. One of his past girlfriends may be an art counterfeiter. Kevin possibly fathered several children in his pursuit of his carnal lusts. And so far, he was a con man of the first order!" she responded with a sigh.

"But did Sassafras kill him?" Mickey asked.

"I can't truly say. One way or the other, Sassy had a motive. But so did a lot of other people, and we still don't have a complete list of suspects yet."

Darcy's intercom buzzed, and she pushed the button. "What is it?"

"Millicent Cooper is on line two, Mrs. Bower," the voice said.

Darcy pushed the button on line two. "Hey, Millie. What's up?"

"I got some financials on Dr. Wilson, and I'm working on those guys that Susan Baxter told us about. Wilson's dirty. The investors, Hollis and Grayson, look clean, but we should talk with them anyway, just to get their take on Kevin."

Mickey raised a hand in a goodbye wave, and softly said, "We'll catch up later when you're free."

She nodded her head back at him and continued talking to Millicent. "We have a couple of hours before the end of the day. Let's talk to Wilson. I'll be there to pick you up in a few minutes!"

Thirty minutes later, Darcy pulled into the driveway of Millie's home. She bounded out of the car and into Millie's house, heading straight for the den. "Hey, Millie. First let me see those financials you have on Wilson," she called out as she walked in the room.

Millicent motioned for Dracy to join her at the countertop between the den and the kitchen. She had a laptop and paper scattered around the counter.

"Hey, get the rest of the printouts over there off the printer," Millie said, pointing at the printer in the far corner of the room.

Darcy picked them up and went back to the countertop. Millicent shut down the computer and looked at Darcy. She pointed to the stack of papers on the counter.

"Look at that stack," she said. "Wilson had a nice cash deposit to his personal bank account around the time of Mrs. Riggles' death. As a matter of fact, it was two days after the good doctor signed the death certificate stating her death as suicide. I got her complete medical records from the hospital back ten years from her death."

"And?" Darcy inquired.

"And she was in perfect health, except that she had recently had an abortion. Father unknown, because there was no DNA test done on the fetus. It was assumed that Mr. Riggles was the father. I also ran medical on him too. He had a vasectomy over twenty years ago."

"We knew that. Sort of...." Darcy stated.

"I also got copies of the Bridgeton Newspaper that reported her death as a suicide. The article reported she suffered from early-onset Alzheimer's, which led to her depression, which drove her to suicide."

Darcy looked at her openmouthed. "That was during the time Riggles was running for city council."

"Yep. It was. If the authorities ruled her death a murder, the public would have demanded an investigation into him and his background. Most certainly, it would have exposed her affair with Kevin, and that would have put a kibosh on his campaign," Millicent gave Darcy a sardonic smile. "But a suicide as a result of his loving wife's illness would cause public sympathy and gain him votes."

"Maybe so, but he didn't get elected," reflected Darcy.

"For many businesspeople, even when you don't get elected, you win. In a small town like this, the position is only part time, but your name gets out there. It's like cheap advertising, whether you win or lose. Businesses get more customers. Lawyers get more clients, and doctors get more patients. It was no different for Lawrence and Riggles. Their business boomed. He is with one of the largest law firms in the city now, and his growth began right after her death."

"Let's go have a little talk with Dr. Wilson, and then when we get back, you can run some financials on Riggles," Darcy said as she got up.

"Yep, I'll get right on it when we get back. And we are taking the Lambo, girlfriend."

Darcy rolled her eyes. Millicent gave her a huge grin.

Millicent was quiet on the way to Wilson's home and drove at a respectable speed. Darcy knew Millie was deep in thought about what she had found.

As she pulled into the driveway of the Wilson's estate, she shut the engine off, and turned to Darcy. "I bet you anything that Riggles paid Wilson to change that report," Millie said as they got out of the car.

"I believe you're right," answered Darcy.

Darcy rang the bell, and an older man with white shorts and a polo shirt answered the door. When he saw the two women, he smiled. "Hello, ladies. How may I be of service to you?"

"We're here to talk to you about Mrs. Riggles' autopsy report," Millicent said, holding up the stack of printouts.

"That was over two years ago. I don't know what there is to talk about," he answered.

"May we come in?" asked Darcy.

"No. We have nothing to talk about. That is a closed case," he stated.

"Take a look at this," Millicent said as she pulled up a bank statement that showed bank deposits of five-figure amounts.

"Where did you get that?" he blasted.

"Let us in, and we'll discuss it," Millicent said with a bold smile.

He stood motionless for a few moments.

"Well? Are we coming in to talk, or do we leave for the District Attorney's office and tell them what we have here?" pressed Millicent.

"I guess you can come in." He stepped aside and let them in. "Straight back to the right."

They went to the back of the home and went to the right as he directed. They entered a large room with a high ceiling and several skylights, and a pool table in the middle of the room. Around the table were pictures of horses and jockeys in full uniform. They also saw pictures of the doctor standing beside horses with their jockeys holding trophies.

"I see you are a horse lover," Millicent said.

"Yes. I like horse racing. I care nothing about horses," he said dryly.

He put out a hand, directing them to several overstuffed chairs around a table. They could see it was one of those tables that could have the top removed to expose a card table. It was probably used for regular home games of poker or some other form of gambling game.

Millicent placed the stack of paper on the tabletop in front of a chair and sat down. Darcy sat beside her. The doctor took a seat on the other side of the ladies.

"Why are you here?" he asked.

Darcy spoke up. "We want to know why you signed Janet Riggles' death certificate as suicide. The facts shown in the autopsy show plainly that it was murder. I'm not a doctor, and even I can see that!"

"It is none of your business why I did that. And you can't prove it wasn't suicide," defended his actions.

"When we get another medical examiner to look at the report, they will plainly see the results speak for themselves. Here is a copy of her complete medical background. There are no reasons or health issues there that would indicate she had Alzheimer's. There are plenty of indications that it was strangulation. Do you want to explain that?" Millicent added.

"I don't have to prove anything to you. You aren't medical professionals."

"True, we aren't, but we want to know why you suddenly deposited one hundred and fifty thousand dollars into your account two days later. Then we saw it was wired out within twenty-four hours. Where is that money now?"

"I don't know how you got those documents, and my personal banking records, but however you got them, it was illegal. You can go to jail for that!"

"No, we won't. We don't know where it came from. Private messenger to her office delivered it," Millicent said with a wicked smile as she pointed at Darcy.

"Somebody gave it to you, and you know who!" he said.

"Nope. No idea. It just appeared on her desk this afternoon," Millicent laughed. "Now, do you want to tell us who sent the money to you, or should we proceed to the District Attorney's office and give this to him and tell him about the delivery messenger that gave the information to us!"

He sat breathing heavily. "What do you want?"

"A name. That's all. If you give us a name, and the name checks out, all of this will disappear. At least your complicity goes away," said Millicent.

"It will go away completely?" he asked, now thoroughly defeated.

"Yes, gone," Millicent answered again.

"How do I know you'll not come back and blackmail me for more later?" He asked.

"We don't care why you did it. We just want to find her killer at this point. You didn't kill her, you just protected the person who did. Now you will help us find that person," Darcy spoke up.

"We're trying to find Janet Riggles killer. That may lead to the person who was killed last week," Millicent said.

He narrowed his eyes. "You mean Kevin Samson? Didn't they arrest the physically disabled woman who runs the gas station convenience store for that crime?"

"Yes. That woman has a name. She is Sassafras Magill, and she didn't kill Samson."

"We have investigated Samson enough to know he deserved to die, but she didn't do it."

"How is she connected to the murder of Janet Riggles?" he now seemed interested.

"We can't go into all that, but we want to clear Magill's name. Your only connection to any of this is that you protected a killer. We don't know, but maybe the same person who killed Mrs. Riggles killed Kevin Samson," said Darcy.

"So, you will not report me for what I did?" he pleaded.

"We will not call the DA on two conditions," stated Darcy.

"Here it comes. How much do you want?" he took a deep breath and asked.

"First, we want the name of the person who sent you the check," Darcy said. "Then we want a check for $150,000, payable to Bridgeton's Children's Benevolent Fund."

"What? I don't have that money anymore. It's gone!" he breathed.

"You shouldn't have lied. We want nothing for ourselves. We want it for the children," added Millicent. "I think by the end of the week is enough time."

"That gives me only a few days. I can't get that much that soon."

"It will take me at least thirty, maybe forty-five days to get that kind of cash."

"We don't care, Doc," Millicent said.

Darcy spoke up. "We aren't totally heartless. You can have until the end of the week to get twenty-five thousand. Then twenty-five thousand each week until the entire amount is paid in full."

"I can't get that much. I swear I can't. I don't have it," he pleaded.

Millicent riffled through her stack of paperwork. "Sure, you can. You have six accounts here scattered around. They total over half a million dollars, Doctor. I suggest you consolidate some of that money. If you think we're stupid, here's a list of the accounts, complete with the account numbers. Since we have the numbers, we could do it for you, but really, we want nothing for ourselves. If you do it, you can even count the donations off as a tax deduction. How about it, Doc?"

Millicent handed him the page she had read from. She gave him another of her evil smiles. "You could do it by this weekend, but as we said, we aren't heartless. Just do it on schedule, and you will never hear from us again. If you don't, you will hear from the DA."

He stood looking at the page in his hands. He looked up at them. Now they were both smiling.

"Do we have a deal?" Millicent asked.

"Yes."

"Good. Now, who bribed you to sign the death certificate as suicide?" said Millicent as she stared intently at him.

"It was Jonathan Riggles. He said it would help his campaign for city council. I'll get you the money. Just don't tell John I gave you his name."

"We agree not to tell him where we got it, but at some point, we'll let him know we have it. That's all we can promise. Now, see how easy that was? We still have a copy of every page. I may be one gorgeous blonde, but I'm not stupid, doctor." Millie got up and motioned for Darcy to follow. Both ladies went to the front door and walked out.

When she turned back, Doctor Wilson was standing almost at attention at the door. Millie blew him a big kiss and gave him a wink. They both got in the car and fired it up. She burned rubber as she squealed out of the long driveway leading to the street.

As Millicent drove down the street, Darcy mused for a few seconds and said, "An anonymous delivery person did not deliver that paperwork you had there to my door."

Laughing, Millicent answered. "Yes, it was. It was delivered after you left the office to come to my house. I had it delivered to protect us. It's called 'plausible deniability.'"

"I know what it's called. I just never thought about it."

"If we get caught getting private documents, we could be held liable. It's an invasion of their privacy, and we could be fined for it. By the way, a court cannot use any of that because whoever got it did so illegally."

"How do you know all this stuff, Millie?"

"Ask me no questions, I'll tell you no lies. Remember, plausible deniability, girlfriend."

They rode on in silence until they got back to Millicent's home. "That's about it for the day," said Darcy as she got out of the car. "I really must get to work early tomorrow and get some actual work done on the real estate before I get back on this project."

"Yeah, I'm getting behind in my television watching. They're having a Humphrey Bogart movie marathon all this week. Hey, in what movie did Bogart say, 'Here's lookin' at you, kid?'"

"Millie, I don't know, and I don't care," Darcy said as she closed the car door.

As she turned to go to her car, she heard Millicent call out to her, "It was Casablanca."

"Still don't care, Millie!" she called back as she reached her car.

CHAPTER FOURTEEN

A young man came into the store that morning and purchased a cup of coffee and a breakfast sandwich. Sassy was working the register that morning, so she checked out the guy, and he went over to the small table in the corner and sat. Sassy made his sandwich and took it to the table.

"How are you doing, Miss?" he asked.

"I'm fine. I hope you like the sandwich," Sassy said.

"I'm sure I will. I've been buying my gas here for several months, but I've never come inside. I usually pay at the pump."

"That's what most people do. Pay at the pump, I mean. We have a few regulars that come inside."

He took a bite, chewed, and looked at Sassy. "What's your name?" he said.

"It's Sassy Magill. What's yours?" she returned the question.

"It's Tony. You own this place, don't you?"

"Yes. I took it over when my parents retired," she said.

"Do they still live in town?"

"Why all the questions, Tony?"

"I don't know. I was hoping to get to know you better. That's all."

"Okay. I understand that, but why now, if you've been coming here for months to fill up with gas?"

"Well, I heard you were kind of cute, but you had a boyfriend. So, I never came in."

"Thanks, but who told you that?"

"Just some friends."

"How long have you lived here in Bridgeton?" she asked.

"Just a few months. I don't have a girlfriend yet," he said shyly.

She laughed. "But you're looking?"

"Yeah, kinda." He looked down at the paper plate that held what was left of his breakfast sandwich.

"And you thought maybe I needed a boyfriend?"

"I heard you broke up with your boyfriend. I mean, he broke up with you."

"You think I need another one?"

"Ah, yes.... I mean no. I don't know what I mean. I'm not very good with girls. That's all. I'm sorry. I think I need to get to work now. Goodbye," he said as he got up to leave.

As he neared the door, Sassy called out to him, "Hey, Tony. What time is your lunch?"

"It's twelve thirty to one thirty," he answered.

"We'll have lunch. Pick me up, and we'll have lunch at Pizza Heaven down on Main Street. We each pay our own bill."

He hesitated and then smiled. "Okay, thanks. See you at half past noon." He walked out the door whistling

When she turned, Jamie and Reilly were both looking at her. Jaime had a big smile on her face. "Sassy has a date," Jaime said.

"It's not a date. It's only lunch. Now, everyone, back to work."

The morning went well, and she was happy and looking forward to her lunch date.

CHAPTER FIFTEEN

❧

Millicent dragged into Darcy's office. "Hey girl, what are you working on today?"

"I'm working on a proposal for a bank loan to renovate some property."

"How much this time?" Millicent asked as she yawned.

"I don't have an accurate amount yet, but it will be around four point five million," Darcy answered.

"Dollars?"

"Yes. What do you think I'm talking about? Pesos? Wake up, Millie. Have you done any research on Jonathan Riggles?"

"Yes, but I have found nothing yet. His deep net accounts are all in order. The hundred and fifty thousand doesn't even show up. I even checked his escrow accounts he uses to put client funds in. There were some wire transfers, but not in that amount."

"What if he split it up into several amounts to disguise them, so ordinary bank audits won't detect them?" Darcy asked.

"I don't get what you mean," pondered Millicent.

"Think of several accounts being like branches on a tree. They all reach out in different directions, but all eventually lead to the main trunk. It is like corporations that hide behind audits by setting up holding companies. They're hard and time-consuming but not impossible to trace back to a central source," explained Darcy.

"I think I'm getting the picture, Dee. Corporations use holding companies to obscure their structure."

"Exactly. Riggles set up an escrow account to hold money for ABC company. He sends thirty thousand to that account, which forwards it to another and another. Now he sends twenty thousand to a second company, which does the same, and then a third, and so on until he eventually sends one hundred fifty-thousand to an offshore account that sends it to Doctor Wilson. Then it's almost untraceable by normal means. We can see it deposited, but there is no way to trace it to its source. And it's split up at the source, so it's impossible to prove it from that end. There is no direct link from one end to the other."

"That's a lot of work," sighed Millicent.

"It is a lot of work, but it's a way of hiding money. It's not a good way to launder money, but a great way to hide it. If Wilson's ever audited, it'll show up, and he'll have to explain where it came from. It's to his benefit to claim it on his taxes as income. The government will take the taxes and leave him alone. If he says that he got it from Riggles, they can audit Riggles and may never make a connection. Riggles is safe, but not Wilson."

"Oh, my, what a terrible tangled web they have weaved, or woven. Which is it?" laughed Millicent.

"I have no clue which it is. But I have some sources available to track it. I'll get to my source later. Until then, give me about an hour and I'll be ready to go," Darcy said, picking up the phone. She dialed and waited for Mickey Ray to answer.

"Hello, Dee. How is that proposal coming along?" he said as he picked up the receiver.

"Good morning to you, my favorite brother," she said to him.

"Uh oh. You must want something. You always do when you call me your favorite brother. Do you need more time on the proposal?"

"No. I need Valerie."

"Why do you need her?"

"As you know, Millie and I are trying to find Kevin Samson's murderer."

"How can Valerie help with that?"

"There are some discrepancies among our suspects. We need to find out whether any of them have offshore accounts. We need to know where and what their balances are, and any connections with each other," Darcy explained.

"Got it. If they have any, Valerie will find them for you. Do you want me to relay the information to her, or do you want to tell her yourself?" he asked.

"If I can talk to her, and if she has questions, I can answer them directly."

"Okay, I'll call her, and she'll call you right back, Dee," he said and hung up.

As soon as he hung up, her phone rang, and she knew Valerie had listened to the entire conversation she and Mickey had. Darcy answered.

"Hello, Valerie. How are you today?" she asked.

"I'm doing fine as always, Darcy Jean. How are you?" Valerie asked.

Valerie was an artificial intelligence program that assisted Mickey Ray. A Japanese firm wrote it to assist clients at an exclusive private spa. It had become sentient and continued to assist Mickey after he left the spa. Mickey had named it Valerie after his fiancée. It is self-learning and sometimes enlists other computer systems in problem-solving situations. The computers in Valerie's network could research global projects and find information you can't find anywhere else. It was lightning fast and could gather information faster than the fastest government computers.

Darcy gave Valerie a list of names and information and asked her to find any hidden accounts of everyone on the list. And give her a printout of links and connections anyone has with anyone else on the list.

Valerie remained silent for several seconds to calculate how long it would take her and her other computer assistants to gather the needed information. Darcy waited for Valerie to finish the calculations.

Finally, Valerie said, "Darcy, I know you are there. I can hear your breathing on the phone."

Darcy smiled at herself. "Yes, Val, I was breathing into the phone. How long will it take you to get the information I need?"

"It will take my assistants an estimated time of 46 minutes and 38 seconds from when you authorize the search and compilation of the information. If you want a full-size printout of the information showing possible connections, I will need a full-size architectural printer. There is one located in the architectural and design room at the end of your main hallway. If you want this, it will take an additional 13 minutes and ten seconds."

"Thanks, Valerie. Let me know before you print it out. I want the standard information on my personal office computer. The large printout is private, and I want to be there and remove it before anyone in that office sees it."

"I understand, Darcy. Are you giving me authorization to research this information?"

"Yes. I give you authorization, and it is private information for my eyes only. Understand?"

"I understand. I will proceed. You may begin the time sequence now. If the time needed exceeds or is shorter than my first estimate, I will notify you. It is my pleasure to be of service to you, Darcy Jean Bower."

The line went dead. Darcy called Millie back to her office.

"Did you get in touch with your private source?" Millie asked when she walked into the room.

"I did."

"Okay, what now?" Millie asked.

"We go to see Satchel Hollis. He has 150,000 reasons to want Samson dead," Darcy said. As they walked to the elevator, "For the record, no, we aren't taking the Lambo today!"

"Oh, poo," Darcy heard Millie say behind her.

They drove out of the city limits of Bridgeton and into the surrounding countryside. They continued driving on a small two-lane back road until they saw Hollis Estate and Ranch on a sign beside a paved driveway off the road. Darcy turned onto the road. In the distance, she could see a huge white country estate house with four white fluted columns and tall evergreen trees surrounding the house.

Darcy pulled up to the front door and parked the car. As they sat and looked up, the front door opened and an elderly man stepped out. He was slim, and his silver hair was thinning due to age. He was well tanned and healthy, and he obviously took great care of himself. Darcy guessed him to be around sixty-five or maybe younger. He was wearing a pair of white shorts and a green polo shirt with a prominent logo embroidered on the front. In the bright sunlight, it was hard to miss the bright rings on his fingers and the gold Rolex watch on his wrist. He smiled and motioned for them to come in.

As they got out of the car, he walked up to them. "Good afternoon, ladies. How can I help you?" he said with a bright smile showing bright, perfectly aligned teeth.

As they got out of the car, Darcy called to him, "Are you Mr. Hollis?"

"Yes, but call me Satchel. It's still early enough that we can have a mimosa around the pool in the back. I'm always thrilled when beautiful women visit me."

Millie got out of the car, and whispered, "Hey, Dee, I like him already. Old, rich, and a gentleman to boot!"

They followed him into the house and through it to the kitchen. Stopping at the pitcher on the counter, he took two glasses out of the cabinet. With tongs, he dropped a few ice cubes from a silver ice bucket on the counter and poured a drink into each one. He handed Darcy and Millie each one and then proceeded to the back patio area. He did this without saying a word. When they sat in some metal padded chairs, he looked up at the glowing sun and took a deep breath. He raised his glass and made a toast. "To God our creator and ruler of this world. We thank him for his gift of kindness and grace."

All three clinked their glasses together.

"Now, ladies. How can I help you?"

Millie spoke first. "Well, Mr. Satchel, we need to talk to you about Kevin Samson. Do you remember him?"

He thought for a moment, rubbed his chin, and took a drink of his Mimosa. He smacked his lips, narrowed his eyes, and spoke. "Yep, I remember him. He convinced me to invest in a new company. The idea of the company was good, and the prospectus was well prepared. Everything looked good. But I didn't look deep enough. The company folded, and all the investors lost their money. It was a flop. I lost a hundred and fifty thousand dollars."

"That doesn't upset you, Mr. Satchel?" asked Darcy.

"Satchel, not Mr. Satchel. Just Satchel. Of course, it upsets me. That boy convinced me to give him a lot of money. Then he disappeared. But to be honest, it's my fault. Not his. The first rule of investing is, you should never invest money you can't afford to lose. Win some, lose some. What bothered me is that when the company went under, he didn't have enough consideration to tell me to my face. He just disappeared."

"How long ago was that?" asked Darcy.

"I don't know exactly. It was a year or two, I guess."

"You haven't heard from him recently?"

"Nope."

"What would you do if he knocked on your door?" asked Darcy.

"I would tell him how disappointed I was that he didn't face me when things went south. Because of that, I would never invest with him again. A man has to have some integrity to admit his mistakes."

Millie looked around. "Do you live alone here? This is a big house."

"Oh, no. My wife is in town doing some shopping for dinner. Can I ask you to stay for dinner? We don't get much company. Hey, I don't even know your name?"

"Sure. We would love to stay..." Millie started to say.

Darcy interrupted, "We can't. We really have a lot of work to do the rest of the day, Satchel. It is a wonderful invitation, and we thank you."

Millie put on a sad face. "Aww, spoilsport, Dee. We can work later."

Darcy gave her 'the look' and Millie turned away like a spoiled child.

"I got it. It's almost noon, eat. How about lunch? We're having grilled roast beef sandwiches, and it goes great with a red table wine," he suggested.

"Well..." Darcy said.

"Oh, come on. He's right. We have to eat. Let's stay for lunch," pleaded Millicent.

"Okay," Darcy relented.

"That's wonderful. I'll call Doris and tell her we have guests for lunch. She'll hurry home to meet you. What are your names again?"

"Mine is Millicent Cooper. Call me Millie. Hers is Darcy Jean Bower. Her friends call her Dee."

Satchel picked up the phone on the table where he was sitting and dialed. "Hello, honey. Two very pretty young ladies have stopped by the house and are having lunch with us. When will you be home? In the driveway? That's wonderful. Come on back when you park the car. I'll ask Hazel if she'll bring in the groceries after she prepares our sandwiches."

He clicked the phone off and got up. "I have to tell the maid you are staying for lunch. And let her know to make two more sandwiches." He went into the house, and they heard him calling for Hazel.

Darcy's phone buzzed, and she answered it. She listened for a few seconds, and without a word, clicked off.

"What was that?" asked Millie

"It was my contact. She said the information I asked for is ready, and she is ready to print the large chart when I tell her. We can stay for lunch, but we need to leave as soon as it's polite to go."

Satchel walked back out the door with an older woman by his side. "Hello, ladies. Satchel tells me you came here asking about Kevin Samson."

"Yes, we did, and he was very open about it," said Millicent, looking up at the woman.

"Good," she said and put out her hand for a handshake. "I'm Doris. It's nice to meet both of you. He says you are Millie, and she is Dee. Correct?"

"Yes, ma'am," answered Millie.

"Don't ma'am me," Doris said as she sat down with a mimosa in her other hand. She leaned over and whispered to them, "Satch had to make a bathroom run. When you get old like us, that is a more frequent thing. We refer to it as the age of frequency."

"That's TMI," Darcy thought to herself. She didn't need to know the personal routines of anyone, especially a stranger.

"So, what did Satchel tell you about Kevin?" Doris asked. "That man talks way too much!" she laughed.

"He told us that you invested in a startup company that went broke and that you lost your investment. Not much else," stated Darcy.

"Yep, that's it in a nutshell. I told Satch not to give that boy any money, but Kevin was a charmer, he was. He could sell refrigerators to Eskimos, I declare," she said with a deep Southern accent.

"It seems he really was. Too bad for him. He actually went to law school, graduated and passed the bar. Kevin could have been a brilliant lawyer," Millie said.

"That's what I heard. Oh, here comes Hazel with our sandwiches," Doris said.

Satchel was following behind her. "Thank you, Hazel," he said as he sat down.

Hazel was rolling a serving cart toward the table. She quickly moved the plates from the cart to the table. She picked up the pitcher of mimosas and filled Doris and Satchel's glasses. Darcy and Millicent waved her off on the refill. She then pointed to a pitcher of water.

"Yes, thank you. Water will be fine for both of us," Darcy responded.

After silently placing two glasses of water in front of them, she rolled the cart away.

"She doesn't talk much, does she? Is Hazel an Asian name? She's Asian," noticed Millie.

"Yes. She came to us about a year ago. She speaks some English, but doesn't feel comfortable around people, so she only speaks when it is required of her to serve."

"I see. Does she live in town?" asked Darcy.

"No. We have a small guesthouse over there," Satchel said, pointing to the other side of the pool. "She lives there. That way she has private living quarters."

"Does she do your grocery shopping for you?" Millie chimed in.

"Oh, no. We do all of that. When she's not working in the house, she stays at her own house. Doesn't she, Satch?"

He nodded as he took a bite of his sandwich.

"These sandwiches are wonderful. Aren't they, Millie?" who also nodded her head to Darcy in agreement and with a mouthful of food.

"Thank you. Hazel has learned to cook most American dishes since she's been with us," said Doris.

"How did you find her?"

"Well, Dee, we went through an employment agency in New York. They specialize in immigration and domestic help," said Doris.

Darcy looked around at the house, pool and garden. "What kind of work are you in, Satchel?"

"A little bit of this, some of that. I import some things and export others. I'm mostly retired now."

Doris placed her hand on Satchel's arm and patted it. "He doesn't like to talk about his work. It was very stressful. He had a heart attack, and so he retired. Didn't you, dear?"

He again nodded his head and continued eating between sips of his drink.

Darcy leaned forward, placing her empty glass on the table. "It has been delightful visiting with you, but we must be going now."

"Yes, we have some other things to do, but we thank you for your hospitality, Doris, and you too, Satchel," added Millie.

Darcy and Millicent got up to leave. Satchel got up also to walk them back to the car. After they got in and left, Darcy spoke up, "What did you get out of that?"

"Something's not right," Millie mused. "He was very talkative, but you notice how Doris put her hand on his arm. It was a subtle reminder for him to stop talking. They're doing something."

"I agree. And Hazel. I bet she is an illegal," Darcy added.

"Yep. We should check her out."

"That's easier said than done, Millie."

"Maybe so, but we can try," Millie said.

They rode on in silence, each with their own private thoughts. Finally, Darcy turned off at the Mercury Blvd exit from the interstate.

"Where in the world are we going now?" asked Millie as she sat up in her seat.

"We are going to interview Gary Grayson."

"I don't want to do that now. I want to go home," Millie whined.

"Gary works at the Newport News Shipyard. He'll be getting off work now. We can't see him any earlier in the day," Darcy said.

"Oh, crap. I didn't know you were going to keep me out all night!"

Darcy shot Millicent a quick glance. "All night? It's only 4:30 in the afternoon. Get a grip, girl."

"Yeah, whatever!"

Darcy drove into a housing development in Hampton and parked the car in front of a small house. It was a nice little house, well maintained, with a small, detached garage. In front of the garage was an old car setting on jack stands and undergoing repairs. In the driveway was a five-year-old pickup truck and a small SUV that was probably the family car. The wife probably used it to ferry children to and from school and school events. They looked at each other. It was the home of an average working-class family. They felt sad for this family. Kevin had cheated them out of money they couldn't afford to lose. It takes a special cold-hearted person to prey on these kinds of people.

Each took a deep breath and got out of the car. Millie said in a whisper, "I feel somewhat overdressed to be in this neighborhood."

"You are overdressed. But these people are the backbone of our country. It's hard-working people like these that make this country great. They deserve our utmost respect."

"Well, excuse me, Miss uppity pants," Millie retorted.

"I'm not uppity. My parents started in a neighborhood just like this. Dad worked hard so we could move out. That's all. But I remember living in a house like this when I was a little girl. My dad even worked on his own trucks, like the one in this driveway. I just remember my roots, that's all," Darcy said as she knocked on the front door.

A small woman with a baby on her hip answered the door. "Umm, hello. Can I help you?" she asked.

"Yes, ma'am. Is Gary home from work yet?"

"Yes, he is. Can I help you?" she asked, rocking the baby by swinging her hips back and forth.

"We need to talk with him about a person he may have done some business with a while back," Darcy said.

"Can I ask what it's about?"

Millie was looking around the small living room. "Yes. It's about an investment he made a couple of years ago."

"I don't know about any investments Gary made, but I'll get him for you," she said and turned to go down a hallway off of the living room.

They heard her talking to someone. Then a male voice answered back and said he would be right out.

She came back and offered them a seat on the couch. It was small, and there were a few toys on the floor, but it was clean. There were family pictures on the walls, and a rocking horse pulled into a corner of the room.

"How did you hurt your wrist?" Darcy asked about the small bandage on her arm.

"Oh, that. I was cleaning the floor and knocked a bottle onto the floor, and it broke into a million pieces."

"Yes, I understand how things like that happen," Darcy said. "What's the baby's name?"

"Her name is Anne, after my mother," she said with a smile. "My name is Karen Anne, and we named her Anne Marie. We also have a little boy. He just started preschool. His name is Coleton, after my father."

"That is so sweet that you named your children after your parents. Where do they live?"

The mother looked down at the floor and softly said, "They both died in a car accident a few years ago. We still miss them."

"I'm so sorry the hear that," Darcy answered. "My mother was killed in a car crash a few years ago, so I know how you feel."

At that moment, a tall young man came into the room. He was about medium height, with a head full of dark hair. He was still in his messy work clothes. His jeans were stained with grease and frayed in areas where the equipment he used had rubbed against his pants. He had scrubbed his face, but his hands still had ground-in stains and grease. He was holding a hand towel and was wiping his hand dry. "Hi. What do you need to talk to me about?" He reached out to shake Darcy's hand and immediately withdrew it. "Sorry," he said as he turned his hand face up to show the grease stains on them. "It's one of the results of most shipyard workers. The grease just doesn't come off easily."

Darcy started, "It's okay. We won't take up much of your time, Gary. I'm Darcy Jean, and this is my friend, Millie. We just want to ask you a few questions about Kevin Samson?"

"Sorry, I don't know a Kevin Samson," he said.

Millie spoke up. "How about Kevin Daniels?"

His eyes furrowed, and he looked at his wife. "Karen, why don't you take Anne to play on the swings outside?" he suggested.

She sensed something was wrong. "Gary. Who is Kevin Daniels?"

"It's nobody, Honey. Just take Anne outside, please."

"No. You tell me who Kevin Daniels is, Gary. Tell me right now. Why are these ladies asking about him?" Karen turned to Darcy and asked, "Who is Kevin Daniels?"

Millie and Darcy looked at each other. They instantly knew they had plowed right into a hornet's nest. Darcy and Millie stood up and started to leave.

"Maybe we came at a bad time. We can come back if it's more convenient."

"No, you stay and tell me who Kevin Daniels is. He's some investment person, isn't he?"

Darcy stood, saying nothing.

"Well, is he or not?" Karen looked straight at Darcy.

"Yes. He is."

"I knew it. I knew that's what happened to our money. You gave it to that con man, didn't you, Gary?"

"I... umm."

"Don't lie to me. You gave him all our savings. You stupid man! I hate you, Gary Grayson! I hate you."

She turned to Darcy and Millie. "When that guy came here, I told Gary not to give him any money. We couldn't afford it. Do you see this cracker-box house we live in? We saved that as a down payment on our own house. This shoebox we're renting is only two bedrooms. We need a three-bedroom house. I checked our savings balance a couple of weeks ago, and there was only five hundred dollars in it. What can we buy with five hundred dollars down? We can't even afford a down payment on a used car!"

Gary looked defeated. "He said that by the end of the year, we would triple our money. The company was going nationwide, and their windows would revolutionize the window industry. He promised!"

Again, Karen turned to Darcy and Millie. "Are you here to give us money?"

"No, we're here to tell you that Kevin Daniels is dead," Millie said calmly.

"Great. That's just great. Now we'll never see a red cent of that money. Why didn't you tell me, Gary? Why? Did you think I'd never find out? I've known it for months, but I was hoping someday you would have the balls to face me and tell me!" she screamed.

Darcy and Millie stood up and walked out the door, got in the car and carefully drove away.

"Okay, what did we learn from them?" asked Millicent.

"She was lying," answered Darcy.

"Why do you say that?"

"She said she had checked the bank account a couple of months ago. Do you know of any wife who would not confront their husband immediately if ten thousand dollars went missing from their bank account?"

"You caught that one too," Millie said.

They drove home in silence.

"Millie, do you want to go by the office and see the printouts on the accounts that Valerie found for us?"

"No. I want to go home," she said.

"Your car is at my office."

"Oh, crap. Okay. We can look at the printouts. Dang it, these long days are going to kill me!"

"Late days? Girl, it's only 7:30. You stay up half the night, and it's barely dark outside."

"Yeah, yeah, yeah. Whatever!"

"Seriously, you can go home if you want to, but I'm going to at least look at them."

"Okay. I'll stay too. Are they ready now?"

"No, Valerie won't print them out until I tell her to," Darcy told her.

"Can you call ahead and have them ready?"

"I could, but I don't want anyone else to see them. We should be the only ones in the building. Everyone has clocked out."

She pulled into her parking space in the underground lot, and they got out and entered the building. When they got there, they proceeded to the design room. Darcy called out to the room in general.

"Valerie. Are you here?"

"I'm here waiting for your order to print, Darcy."

"Print it, Valerie."

Millie looked at Darcy in total awe. "You have a voice activated computer system. That's so cool. I want one! How can I get one of those?"

The large printer in the middle of the room started buzzing, and a blue-colored print started slowly coming out of the printer. It continued to print until it touched the floor, and it stopped. "The job is complete," announced Valerie over the intercom system.

Darcy went over and removed the large print and rolled it up. "Let's take this to my office and look at it."

"That is so cool. Where can I get one of those programs? I like it," Millie said.

"You can find programs like that at many home improvement stores. But then you have to install the corresponding hardware so it'll work."

"I want one just like yours. Where did you buy yours?"

"Ours was custom designed. Never mind that. Let's look at this printout." They both heard the door unlock with a click.

"I want one," Millie said again.

Darcy walked over to her desk and unrolled the blueprint paper and put a weight on each side to keep it from rolling up. It looked like a tree with branches. Instead of branches, there were bank names, account numbers, and customer names, dates when transfers were made. Also shown were the initiation location of the transfers and the recipients, complete with the time and date stamps.

"Oh, my gawd! How did you ever get this? How did your contact get this information? It links every transaction for the past five years. Several of our suspects have multiple accounts that tie them to others. It will take me days to sort it all out. This is incredible."

"Grab those prints over there on my printer. These sheets should save you some time. They should be sorted, and connected and even collated, Millie!"

Millie just stared at the blueprint. She put a finger at one point and followed it to the other side of the print. From the sender to the recipient. "Everything is here, Dee. Everything! I've never seen anything like it in my life!"

"Take it home, and sort it out. And get back to me with the results. Can you do that?"

"Yes, Dee. It'll take me a couple of days, but I can do it."

"Remember, it's top secret. If we get caught with this information, we could be in trouble. Every bit of this is personal and private. We have no right to have it."

"Got it," and she gave Darcy a mock salute. "Mum's the word."

"I'm serious. Secret is sacred."

Millie suddenly got serious. "Trust me. I get it, Darcy."

They went home.

CHAPTER SIXTEEN

Tony picked Sassy up on time, which meant a lot to her. She hadn't dated a lot before she met Kevin but felt that a date should always be on time. He got out, came inside the store and waited until she came out and escorted her to his truck. His truck was a high-rise truck, and he had to help her climb into it. It was fancy inside and outside.

She wouldn't hold this against him. Maybe it was all he had. She decided it was. He couldn't make enough money to support a truck like this and much else. He was polite and courteous as he drove to Pizza Heaven.

He also helped her get out, and they walked inside. A young girl came to their table, and he began giving her an order for the pizza. Sassy noticed that he didn't even ask her what she wanted on it, but maybe he was just nervous.

She spoke up and told the server she wanted a diet soda. He ordered sweet tea. When the girl left, he said, "I'm sorry. I forgot to ask what you wanted on the pizza. I just ordered it."

"It's okay. I'll just pick off what I don't want," she said with a smile.

"Okay. Remind me next time. We can get what you want," he said sheepishly.

"What kind of work do you do, Tony?"

"I'm in construction."

"What kind of construction?"

"All kinds. You know, building houses and stuff."

"What is your job on the houses?"

"I'm a framing carpenter."

After a few more minutes, their pizza came, and they ate with brief conversation. He took her back to the store after lunch, and they split the bill.

When she walked into the store, Jame and Reilly both stopped their work. "How was your date?" Jaime asked, glowing with excitement.

"Okay."

"Are you going to see him again?"

"No, Jamie. I think this was our one and only date."

"Why?"

"Because he is boring, that's why. He could barely carry on an intelligent conversation."

"Was he nice to you?" asked Reilly.

"He was nice, but boring. I don't want to see him again," Sassy said with finality.

Jaime and Reilly went back to work.

CHAPTER SEVENTEEN

D arcy pulled into Millicent's driveway, got out and walked to the door and rang the bell. A few seconds later she heard Millie say, "Come on in, Dee. Door's unlocked."

When she got to the den, she saw papers scattered everywhere. Millie had a pad and pencil and was scribbling things on a yellow legal pad. She pointed to the coffeepot in the corner. "Pour a cup and see what I've found."

Darcy followed instructions and went back to the other end of the counter where they had spread the printout from the previous night.

There was a pile of different colored highlighter pens Millie had used to draw lines from one end to the other to connect transfers from one account to another.

Darcy looked at the multicolored lines stretched over the paper. "They all had offshore accounts and multiple accounts all over the world."

Millicent pointed to one Internet address. "It was called Technotec LLC. That one was a scam site designed for potential investors to send money to various scam start-up companies. It has different doors or areas so you can invest in whatever strikes your fancy. If I like medical innovations, I will go here and invest in research into certain diseases, like cancer or mental retardation. That site claims they invested 85% of all money in research and that you could potentially be rich when they cured the disease you invested in. Of course, zero percent of the money actually applies to the research you stated. Every area claims it is almost ready for a worldwide breakthrough. Can you imagine if you owned stock in the company that discovered a cure for cancer or heart disease? This site claims to monitor every research facility in the world and would automatically buy stock in that company just before the cure is announced. It is like an electronic AI version of insider trading."

She took a deep breath and continued. "What we are seeing here is AutoWindow. If you're just an ordinary guy like our friend, Gary Grayson, we might like to invest in a company that has a product we can buy and hold in our hands."

"I also did a check on AutoWindow. It was a real company, but never quite got the funding to properly design a practical window, so it went belly up. It had a link to Grayson and Hollis."

"Oh, yes. I saw several transfers to these numbers," she said as she rambled around looking for another scrap of paper. "Oh, yeah. Here it is," she said, grabbed it and handed it to Darcy. "Those are transfers to numbered accounts in France and the United Kingdom. They were for one hundred thousand to a bank in France, and two for the same amounts to an account in the UK. We need to trace down the owners of those accounts. I strongly suspect they could be payments for domestic help, if you get my drift. This doesn't even touch the Cayman accounts." Millie smiled and took a huge gulp of coffee. "Yuck, this stuff is nasty. It's cold."

"Want me to warm it up?" She reached for Millie's cup.

"Yes," she continued. "I have connected all the dots, so to speak, but I haven't had the chance to track them all down. There is so much information here."

Darcy filled Millie's cup and handed it back to her.

"I kind of got sidetracked. I started tracking Riggles' accounts. He is in real deep. He has three personal accounts and four escrow accounts. I know it can all be handled with accounting transfers, but it is more confusing if you have multiple accounts rather than data entries in the company books. Each company has its own account. It's not impossible, but difficult, to audit and harder to verify each entry. Rather than sending a single large payment, you can send several smaller payments to various accounts across the country or, as in this case, different countries. Some through legal channels can't be traced at all. Like the Cayman accounts."

"As you know, Millie, I'm an accountant, and you have me confused."

"I'm confused too. I've been up all night, and I've only touched the surface."

"Really? All night?"

"Yep. Me and coffee have stayed the course. I'm ready for breakfast." Millie sat down on a bar stool beside the kitchen counter.

"Want me to whip up some eggs and bacon?" Darcy volunteered, heading for the refrigerator.

"I don't have anything like that in the house. Do you know how much cholesterol is in that stuff?"

Darcy laughed. "I should have known. Let's go to the Diner. Breakfast is on me."

The Diner was a favorite hangout for many people in Bridgeton. Darcy remembered her mother and dad bringing her and Mickey here for meals. It didn't matter now, but it was a family favorite place. She also remembered that the Mongoose team sometimes used the private back room for mission planning. It was also the place Valerie Green, Mickey's fiancée, used to work before she left Bridgeton to go to Oregon to attend culinary school.

They walked in and found a seat in the back corner. On the way back, Darcy stopped and talked to several people she knew who had also been coming to the Diner ever since she could remember.

Polly came over with a pen, and order pad in hand. "Good morning, Darcy. How have you been? You haven't been here for weeks. Mickey was in here just yesterday."

"I'm good, Polly. How've things been going for you? Mickey will be here until you and Martha retire and close this place down."

"I guess you're right. What can I get for you, girls?"

Millie spoke first. "What pastries do you have today?"

"The usual. Warm cinnamon rolls and crème cheese muffins, Millie. Do you want one of each?"

"Sounds good to me, Polly. And I want the strawberry crème cheese."

"You got it, Millie. And a strong pot of coffee for the table," Polly added as she turned to take Darcy's order. After taking Darcy's order, she left for the kitchen.

"First, I don't like that Satchel Hollis. Somethings amiss, Dee."

"I agree, but right now our number one priority is finding Samson's murderer, so we can clear Sassy's name," Darcy said, taking a sip of coffee.

"True, but we can't do that until we have everyone's information. Then we get a connection, and that will give us a motive. Besides, he got what he deserved. He was an all-around con man, and a bad person."

"Maybe so, but Sassy doesn't deserve to pay for someone else's crime, Millie. You know that."

Millie hung her head in mock shame. "Yeah. You're right."

They talked about miscellaneous things until breakfast arrived. Darcy took Millicent home to get some sleep and then went back to her office.

Darcy felt she wanted more information about Satchel Hollis, so she called Monica and asked her to find out all she could about Hollis and his wife. She thought she should have a talk with Sassy, and check on her. Mickey was far too trusting of people. Yes, Darcy trusted her, but it was a murder charge.

CHAPTER EIGHTEEN

Darcy pulled up to the pumps at Sassy's place and filled her car up. She then moved to the side parking area.

When she walked in the front door, she saw Reilly at the register and Jaime sweeping the floor. "Hello, Reilly. How are you today, Jaime?"

Reilly gave his typical one-word answer, "Hi," and continued checking the register. Jaime smiled her huge friendly smile, and said, "Hello, Darcy. I'm fine."

"Is Sassy in the back room?"

Jaime nodded as she spied a can on the bottom shelf just an inch out of place. She bent down and moved it back to its proper place.

Darcy continued to the back room where Sassafras was muttering to herself. "What's going on, Sassy?"

"I'm so mad," she said.

"What's the problem now?"

"Kevin's what's wrong. He ruined my life when he was alive, and even in his death, he's ruining it. I hate what's happening to me. Dee, I try to treat everyone right, honestly and fairly. That SOB took advantage of me, and now that he's gone, my life is in shambles. You and Mickey have been among the few that believe in me."

"The whole town has banded together to support you, Sassy."

"Just this morning, I got a call from my gasoline supplier. They have suspended my account and are demanding I pay the bill in full within five days. They refuse to make any more gas deliveries until I'm paid up. And now I have to pay for deliveries in advance. I have never been late with a payment since I took this place over. Not once!"

"I admit, that sucks. I don't know what to tell you," Darcy admitted. "How big are your tanks?"

"Some of the larger stations have three tanks as much as 20,000 gallons. My tanks are small, 10,000-gallon tanks, and I only sell regular and high test, so I only have two tanks. I sell the gas, then pay the bill for the last fill-up. Now they want the bill paid in full, and payment in advance. If I order fewer than 5,000 gallons, they charge me a delivery fee. I have to close the pumps."

Darcy looked around the stockroom. "I thought that your profit would be from the sale of your groceries and staple items, not the gas."

"It is, but the gas brings them into the store. They stop, fill up, and pick up a six-pack or a loaf of bread and milk. If I don't have gas, they'll just go to the next store and get everything they need, so I need to have gas to entice them to shop here."

"I get it, Sassy. I never thought of it that way, but you're right," Darcy agreed.

"I'll have to let Reilly and Jaime go. Reilly is high enough functioning. He lives alone. Jaime still lives with her parents. They both depend on me for a job. If I let them go, and cut back on my own living expenses, it'll still take me six months to save enough cash to reopen the pumps."

"Let me make a few calls and see what I can do, Sassy."

"I don't know what anyone can do."

"I don't know either. Hey, I've heard you have been on a couple of dates. How's the dating scene?"

"Awful. I've had a few dates. One guy only wanted me as a trophy girlfriend."

"What do you mean by that?"

"I mean, he thought he was being a real humanitarian by dating a disabled girl. He was such a jerk. He actually told me how lucky I was to have a date like him. A couple of others were just losers. One only wanted one thing, and I wouldn't give it to him."

"I can guess what he wanted."

"Yep. Exactly. Too bad things didn't work out with the delivery guy we had when all this thing started."

"Who was that, Sassy?"

"His name's Josh. A very nice guy, but he wanted to pay for everything. I pay my own way."

Darcy leaned against a stack of boxes. "Sassafras, that's the way it works. Let the guy pay. It makes them feel superior. Like he can take care of his woman."

"I don't need anyone to take care of me, Darcy. And men are not superior to me. I may be disabled, but I'm not stupid."

Darcy looked straight into Sassy's eyes. She saw sadness, but a strong young woman. "I don't mean superior intellect, or someone that is more powerful. A man likes to be like a warrior protecting his woman. James, my husband, is a warrior, but he knows that in many ways I'm superior. We are a team. It isn't who is the best. I take care of the finances, but he takes care of me and my kids. I go to sleep under his protection and care. He is my knight in shining armor."

"I see, I think," she mused.

"Men want to be the protectors. They want to impress their woman. Take that jerk that wanted you because you're disabled. I agree. He sounds awful, but in his mind, he was protecting you. He was saving you. Dating you made him feel like a big man."

"You think I should have kept dating him?"

"Oh my, no. Absolutely not. He has an ego problem. I wouldn't give a person like that the time of day.

"You want to fall in love with someone that wants you despite your handicap. Not because of it. But let him come to you. When you find him, don't let him go. Hold on to him for dear life." She looked at her watch. "I've got to go. I've got to make some phone calls."

"Yeah. I've got to place an order so I can get it delivered by Friday."

Darcy left, and Sassy sat on one of the empty wooden boxes in the storeroom. She thought about what Darcy had said. Darcy was smart, married, and had kids. She had a wonderful life. Darcy had what she wanted.

She reached for the phone and dialed. "Hello, Glenda. I need to place a small order. I think it will be over the minimum dollar amount for an order."

"Well, hello, Sassy. Great to hear from you. Dear, you don't have to fill a minimum amount. If you need just one item, there's no delivery charge. What do you need?"

She read off her list, and Glenda said she could have it delivered tomorrow. "Now, the one thing I have to say is, everyone but Josh, has their orders for tomorrow. I'll have to send him. Is that okay with you?"

She hesitated, then sighed. "Sure. Josh will be fine."

"Okay, dear. I'll have him load it onto his truck now. You will probably be the last of his deliveries, so it'll be late in the day."

"That's okay. Thanks, Glenda." Sassy hung up the phone. She didn't know how she felt about seeing Josh again. He was handsome and so polite, but she was stubborn the last time, and maybe she blew her chance with him. She guessed she would find out tomorrow.

As soon as the call disconnected, Glenda pressed the button on the speaker system in the warehouse. "Josh, please come to my office to pick up an order for tomorrow's delivery."

She typed the order into her computer. The printer spit out the order, with all charges, including the waived delivery fees.

Josh walked into the office. "Yes, ma'am. I'll make the delivery, but I already have a full load."

"I know, but I'm switching your route today with Teddy. You run this route tomorrow, and deliver this one last," she said as she handed him the order.

He took one look at it and saw the last delivery was to Sassy's place. "Glenda, I thought I'd asked you to change my route."

"I did, but I changed it back. You now have this route again."

"But I don't feel comfortable with this one anymore."

"Listen Josh. I know you had some kind of disagreement with Sassafras, but she really is a very nice girl. I've known her since she was born. This company was delivering to her parents when they first went into business. She's going through a very tough time right now. Try to mend your fences, and help her, for me. Can you do that as a favor to an old woman... and your boss?"

He looked down at the order in his hand. "Yes, ma'am. I really did like her, but she's kind of..."

"I know, but if you had to deal with the world like she is doing, you might be a bit different too. You won't find a nicer, more independent, and honest person in this whole town as Sassafras Magill."

"Sure. I can do that. She's kind of pretty too. At least, I think she is," he said sheepishly.

"Good boy. Now get out of my office and go to work," Glenda laughed.

Sassy sat on the box in the storeroom and daydreamed. She was kind of looking forward to seeing Josh again, but he may not even want to speak to her the way she talked to him the last time. She didn't know, but she could hope. He was so nice, and she blew him off so rudely. "Oh, well," she thought. "She'd deal with it when he got here."

The following day was long. They worked at the store. Sassy was concerned about how long she could keep the pumps turned on, because she needed the cash flow to keep Reilly and Jaime employed. She had run the store alone when she first took over the store from her parents. But there were certain things that were very difficult physically because of her cerebral palsy. The bending over and placing things on the bottom shelf was terribly hard on her knees and back. When she stocked the shelves, she had to sit on a stool, and it took her all day long to do what Reilly and Jaime could do in two hours. She would make it work. She had to. Maybe she could keep them on for another week.

As they were finishing up, Josh rolled up and walked in with a hand-truck stacked with items. "Hello, Sassy. How have you been?"

She smiled and looked at him. "I'm doing okay. How about you?"

"Good." He saw Jaime and Reilly and made it a point to wave and speak to them as well. "Hi, Jaime. You look cute today."

Jaime smiled back, and then she blushed. "Hi, Josh."

"Sas, where would you like this stuff? It's a smaller order than last time."

She pointed to the back area of the room. "Back there is fine."

"I'll drop this and go back and get the rest of the stuff. I have some time, so I can help you stock it."

"Thank you, but we can do it."

Jaime spoke up, "Let him help, Sassy."

"Yeah, Sassy. Let me help," he added, showing his gleaming white teeth.

"Okay."

He turned around, dumped the items where she pointed. "Great. With all of us, we'll have it done in a jiffy!"

He brought two more hand-truck loads, and they began putting items on the shelves while Jaime went behind each one to position each item in its exact spot.

"How have you been since I saw you last, Sas?"

"Okay, I guess."

"Last time I was here, we almost had a lunch date. Can I still have a chance at that?"

"Are you sure you want to do that?"

"If I hadn't wanted to, then I wouldn't have asked you."

"We go Dutch?"

"Sure, why not. At least I know where I stand," he laughed as he put an item on a shelf.

Jaime clapped her hands and laughed. "Sassy's got a date."

"It's not a date..."

Josh touched Sassy on the shoulder. "Let Jaime enjoy her moment. We can pretend if it makes her happy."

Turning to Josh, "That's very thoughtful of you, Josh," Sassy stated.

"People like her and Reilly deserve whatever it takes to make them happy."

"Yes, they do. Where would you like to meet?" Sassy asked.

"Can I at least pick you up for lunch?"

She couldn't help grinning. "Yeah, I guess that would be okay too. That would make things easier for me," she said, looking down at her twisted legs.

With a mock salute, he returned her grin. "It would almost be like a real pretend date."

When he was gone, she felt almost happy. It was the best she had felt since Kevin had broken up with her. All it took was an almost pretend date, with a nice guy.

When it was closing time, Jaime gave her a big hug. "I'm happy too."

"I know you are Jaime."

"I downloaded everything to the computer for you, Sassafras," called Reilly. "Can I go home now?"

"Yes. You may go home," she called back. "You too, Jamie."

They walked out the door, and she heard Reilly lock the door. That night she slept better than she had slept in weeks.

The following morning, she got up feeling happy, and even her morning stretches seemed easier. Although they were busy, the morning went by so slowly. It was like waiting for Christmas.

Finally, it was noon, and Josh pulled up right on time. He got out and went inside to get her. She walked outside. "Hey, you're driving the delivery truck?"

"Yes, it's my lunchtime. I always eat lunch in the truck. I don't have enough time to go home and switch vehicles."

"I'm sorry. I can't get into that truck. It's much too high for me to step up."

"I'm so sorry. I didn't even think about that. I didn't mean to..."

She cocked her head. "You didn't realize that I'm disabled?" she said with a wink and a smile.

"Well. Yes. I knew that, but I don't think of you as disabled. I'm so sorry, Sassy. I didn't mean..."

This time she laughed out loud. "Stop apologizing. I know what you meant. But I don't like people calling me disabled. I'm handicapped, but I'm not disabled. That implies that I'm not able to do things. I can do almost anything I want. It's just that some things are more difficult than others. But it's sweet that you forget I have limitations. In the future, if we go out, you must consider these things."

"You're right. Wait. I know what. I have a step stool in the back of the truck. I'll get it for you." He rushed around to the back. She heard him open the door and then a metallic clang. He came back to her door and put a two-step stool beside the door.

He held out his hand to her so she could steady herself as she climbed into the truck. "I think it's so sweet that you forgot I'm handicapped."

"I should be more aware of it. When I'm around you, I think of you as a normal person. I'm sorry."

She got serious for a few moments. "Please, Josh. Stop apologizing. I'm honored that you don't consider my limitations. It is a part of me, and if we continue seeing each other, you'll get used to it."

As he started the engine, she could see he visibly brightened. "You mean we may go out again?"

"I said, if we continue seeing each other. We may decide we aren't suited for each other."

"Okay, I'll settle for that now. If you call ahead and order our lunch, I'll drive. Lunch will be ready, so we can eat and still have a few minutes to talk," he said, pulling into the street.

He pulled up to the front door and helped her get out. She checked their order and got a table while he parked.

She asked him if they could ask a blessing before they ate.

He answered her. "Sure. I don't always do it. I just get busy and forget."

She asked for a blessing on the food and both of them. "I always say a blessing. I guess everyone forgets sometimes, but if Jaime and Reilly eat with me, I always ask it. It's setting a good example for them."

"I never thought of that, but you really try to set a good example for them, don't you?"

"Yes. I try."

"So how are things going at the store?"

"Good, but I may have to close in a few weeks. Because of my legal problems, my gasoline supplier has put me on a cash on delivery basis. That is where I make most of my money. It is a convenience store. People come and gas up and get a cup of coffee and a sandwich on the way to work, or a loaf of bread on the way home. They don't do their weekly shopping there. Even for me, the groceries barely break even and pay the utilities. When this load of gas is sold, I will have to let Jaime and Reilly go and work the store alone. I'll have to take more frequent and smaller deliveries. The less I buy, the more it costs."

He reached over and took her hand. "I'm so sorry to hear that."

She shrugged her shoulders. "When I took over the store from Mom and Dad, I worked it all alone, but then I could make it. It is physically difficult for me because of my um..."

"Yeah. I know," he said.

A young kid put the tray on the table with their food and laid the bill beside the tray. "No hurry. Enjoy your lunch."

They ate in almost embarrassing silence. "I have an idea." Josh took a sip of soda to wash down his food.

"Okay?"

"What are your hours?"

"8 AM to 6 PM."

"Great. Now hear me out, okay?"

"Sure."

"If you open at 7 AM and close at 8 PM, you'll get a few more sales. I have to get to work at 6 AM to load the truck. When I get back at around 6 PM, I sweep it out to get it ready to load the following day. Follow me so far?"

"Yes. Where is this going?"

"I'm working full time, but I can ask Glenda if I can go part time for a while, until you get back on your feet."

"That doesn't help at all, Josh. It'll shorten the time I can stay open because I will sell out the shelves sooner. And what does your going part time have to do with anything?"

"I don't go out much so I can help at the store. You take the morning shift from 7 AM to 1 PM. and I'll come in and work till closing."

"Duh! Josh, do you hear yourself? I can't pay my regular help. How could I ever pay you? And I will not let you work without pay! I told you, I pay my way."

"I agree. But I have some money saved up, so I don't need money right now. I'll work on account. Like when you had an account with your suppliers. You have thirty to sixty days to pay the invoice they send you."

"I pay Jaime and Reilly weekly."

"Yes, but I've saved up enough to last for several months. Everything should be cleared up in sixty days at the most, right?"

"I hope so, but I don't have enough money to last over two weeks for payroll. Then, if I don't make enough sales on groceries, I'll have to close the store. You still won't have a job."

"We'll cross that bridge when we get to it. How about it? I'll talk to Glenda this afternoon."

Hesitantly, she sighed. "Okay. I'll think about it. And no more lunches out. I can't afford it."

"I get it. I'll pay for lunch today. It's not free. I'll put it on your account. Due in full in sixty days," he reached over and grabbed the bill. "Hey, girl, lunch is over. This boy's got a job to get back to."

At the store, he helped her get out and drove off with a honk and a wave. She didn't know how she felt, but she was relieved.

CHAPTER NINETEEN

"Dee, have you heard from Sassafras lately? I haven't heard from her in days," came Mickey's voice over the phone when she answered it.

"Yes, Millie and I have been working on her case. Are you worried about her or the bond you put up?"

"In truth, I guess I'm worried about both."

Darcy laughed into the phone. "I thought you trusted her."

"I do, but things happen. People change. You remember Francine. I loved her, and she tried to kill me!"

Getting serious again, Darcy sighed, "Yes. I remember. You have terrible luck with women. I'll check on her today, but I'm sure she's doing fine."

"Thanks. Give me an update later, Sis!"

Mickey was right. A few years ago, he had fallen head over heels in love with the mayor's daughter, and it turned out she had been a stone-cold killer. Darcy picked up the phone and dialed Millicent.

"Hey, Dee!" came Millie's voice over the other end of the line.

"What have you found out?"

"Come on over and I'll tell you."

"Okay, but give me a couple of hours. I have some paperwork I need to get done in the office, and I want to stop by Sassy's Place and see how she's doing."

"Okay. I'll keep digging into these guys. It gets worse the more I dig."

She hung up and sat there thinking. Was Sassafras part of this, or just an innocent bystander? A victim of a very dirty person. She hoped not. The deeper they dug, the dirtier Kevin seemed.

As usual, Jaime was sweeping and rearranging things on the shelves when Darcy walked inside. She wondered how Jaime could do that all day long without going crazy from boredom. Down syndrome people could fixate on a task and do it repeatedly. Reilly was typing at the computer over in the corner behind the register. They are a real asset to Sassy's business. She was lucky to have them.

"Hello, Jaime. Hi Reilly." She knew that when someone, anyone, spoke to Jaime, it made her happy to be recognized. Reilly was in his own world, but Darcy always included him in her greetings. "Where is Sassy?"

"She's in the stockroom," Jaime smiled and pointed.

Darcy walked back and saw Sassy staring at the wall. "What's up, Sassy?"

"Nothing."

Darcy sat down beside her. "I can see that something is wrong. Tell me."

"I'm just worried about what is going to happen. Am I going to jail for the rest of my life? What's going to happen to Jaime and Reilly when I must close the store?"

"First, I must say if you didn't kill Kevin, Millie and I will clear your name. Now, why do you have to close the store?"

She raised her hand. "I swear I didn't kill him. I'm not sorry he's dead, but I didn't kill him."

"Okay, I believe you. Now, why do you have to close the store?"

"Because the gas supplier has closed my credit account." She told Darcy the whole story about the gas supplier again, and her profit margin to run the store. "If I can't work the store alone, I'll have to close the doors."

Darcy sat back in the hard-backed chair and looked at the ceiling. That was a pose she got from Mickey Ray. When he was deep in thought, he would lean back and stare at the ceiling.

Sassy looked at her but didn't break the silence. They sat in total silence for several minutes. Finally, Darcy looked back down at Sassafras. "Here's what I will do. Starting next week, I will give Jaime and Reilly a job until this murder mess is over. I have a cleaning staff that cleans the offices. They work at night, but we can work something out about that. Reilly can set up the register to connect to our computer network. When the store closes, your register can log onto our network and download the day's sales and enter the daily results into a computer log. As you know, I'm head of the accounting department at the company. We can find something for Reilly to do in that department as well."

"I can't let you do that."

Darcy held up her hand in the universal stop motion. "I can, and I will. I'll instruct their supervisors about their limitations to help them adjust to their new jobs. They'll be fine, and they'll earn their pay, so it's no financial burden on us. Now, I'll also ask Mickey Ray to instruct all our company vehicles to fill up here. I'm sorry, but some of our bigger trucks are diesel, and you don't have a diesel pump, so they'll have to continue where they normally fill up. That won't solve all your financial problems, but maybe it'll help you stay open until this is solved."

"Oh, Darcy, you are truly a lifesaver. You're a godsend."

As Darcy got up, she started for the door. "We'll continue to do what we can to help you and find Kevin's actual killer. If you believe in God, you need to pray for us to do our job."

She got in her car and headed for Millicent's home. She also put in a call to Monica. "Monica, I need to send out a bulletin to all employees. If they buy gas for their personal vehicles at Sassy's place and get a receipt for the purchase, we'll give them a rebate of five cents per gallon. This starts today and will continue for 30 days."

"Okay, got it. Can I ask why?" Monica responded.

"We need to support Sassafras Magill."

"That's good enough for me. That girl is getting railroaded. I'll get right on it."

When she pulled into Millicent's driveway, she got out and walked into her house, without knocking as usual. "Millie, tell me what you found out!" she called as she headed for the den area.

As she put her purse down and looked around the room at all the loose papers lying everywhere, she told Millie about Sassy closing the store.

"Aw, I'm sorry to hear that. I'll do my part. I'll start buying my gas from her. And I can start buying at least a few things there to help her out."

"Thanks. Now tell me what's going on here."

"I have found a lot of transfers of Hollis accounts. He moves money around the world. A bank in France and England, but the most interesting ones are the accounts in the Cayman Islands, and a numbered account in Switzerland."

"Where did he get his money?"

"Believe it or not, he won a fifty-million-dollar lottery a few years ago. Slowly, the money has disappeared. Well, not really disappeared, he just split it up all around the world in different banks. He has enough in American banks that no one even considers his other ones. Also, he has several aliases. He can travel incognito whenever and wherever he wants."

"Now, the poor guy, Gary Grayson, he has nothing. Even his credit is bad. I don't even know how he managed to save ten grand to give to Kevin. I'm still looking into that."

Darcy had poured herself a cola while Millicent was filling her in, and she took a drink. "I forgot. This is regular Coke. Where's the diet stuff?"

"In the back of the fridge. You know I get that especially for you! Hey, I can't find Hollis doing anything illegal, but with that kind of money and the way he moves it around, something is rotten in Denmark. Want me to keep looking?"

"Not right now. We need to concentrate on Kevin's killer."

"Yeah, right. Moving on to Mr. Samson or Daniels, if you will. He isn't, excuse me, wasn't the brightest criminal in the network."

"Network?"

"Just an expression, Dee. He has four hundred eighty-nine thousand dollars in an account in London. A third grader with a smartphone could have found that one. Now here is the kicker. Susan Baxter had an account at the same bank. At least she used a different name. She was also easy to track. She transferred money from her bank here to there by wire. The wire connection is how I connected. The name on that account is Sophia Barter. Just close enough that no one will really connect it without some time. As long as she keeps a low profile, no one will know. She has two point six million dollars in her account."

"Whoa! A big difference," exclaimed Darcy.

"Yep, they probably were a team, conning buyers, but she took the bigger half of the cut!"

"She's the sharp knife in that game," said Millicent with a huge smile.

"You did well, my sharp friend!"

"I know. I really am good!" Millie laughed.

"When this is over, we can take Kevin's money out of that bank and return it to Sassy."

"I don't know if I can do that."

"Don't worry about that. I know people. My people know people, and her people..."

"I get the idea, Dee. Who do we look at now? I think we should look deeper into Susan Baxter."

"She's as good as anyone, I guess. Can you get in touch with your friend on the police force and find out what progress they have made on Sassy's case? We both know the first twenty-four hours are the most crucial, and it's been almost two weeks since they booked Sassafras."

Millicent thought for a moment. "I guess I can give him a call. But you know the police. When they get a viable suspect, they don't spend a lot of time on what they consider a waste of time getting to the truth. They don't look for the truth. They look at the conviction rate."

Darcy sighed. "I know. That's why I want you to find out what they're doing now. See if your inside person can get some information on what Detective Halligan is working on."

CHAPTER TWENTY

J osh showed up the following day at 1 PM sharp. "Sorry I couldn't get here any sooner. Glenda was really great about rearranging the schedule to let me back off to part time. Another guy has been wanting more hours. Now he's full time, and I'm part time."

"You aren't due to start for three more days. Jaime and Reilly don't leave until then. They don't start at the Christianson Company until next Monday."

"Hey, I have a great idea. You're closed on weekends, right?"

"Yes, Josh. The pumps are on for credit card gas purchases, but the store is closed."

"There's a county fair this weekend. Let's take the kids to the fair. It'll be fun!"

"Josh, what are you talking about? What kids?"

"Jaime and Reilly. They are kind of like kids, sort of."

"You aren't making fun of them, are you?"

He suddenly got serious. "No. I would never do that. Not in a million years. Mentally, they are at a kid's level. They are young and innocent. They get joy from the simplest things. I like that, and I like them. I want us to share some joy and take them to the fair!"

"Okay, that might be a kind of present to say goodbye to them."

He smiled at her. "It's not goodbye. They'll be back after all this crap is over. The entire day is on me. I have enough money saved to sponsor their day."

"Can I pay my way?" she asked.

"I guess, since you have a thing about that. I won't insist, but I really would like to pay for you too," he said.

"Since you are going to be working for me, I'll just put it on my account."

"That's what I'm talking about! You are officially off duty, and I'm running the store until closing time," Josh said with a grin.

"Okay, I have several loads of laundry to do. I'll be back around closing time to give them their last paychecks, and a little bonus as a parting gift for them." Sassy turned and headed for the stairs to her apartment.

Josh helped Reilly and Jaime with their work. When necessary, he waited on customers by carrying the groceries to the counter so that Reilly could check them out.

At closing time, Sassy came down and gave them their last paychecks and a small bonus. They all hugged and even included Josh in the goodbyes. Sassy assured them that as soon as business picked up again, they would come back and work for her.

Josh told them about the fair and insisted they spend the following day having a good time to remember their time together.

After they left, Sassy locked the door and turned off the pumps. They went back to the stockroom and breakroom to have a cup of coffee to end the day.

Josh took a sip of the hot liquid. "The kids are great workers, and I noticed the customers like them too. I'm sure they'll be missed."

After a couple cups of coffee, and more small talk, he went home.

The following morning, he was at Sassy's place with an old car they all thought would leave parts lying on the road as it traveled along. "Okay, kids. Everyone get out while I go to park the car." He gave Sassy some bills to buy a small roll of tickets for the attractions. When he got back, they all started for the carousel ride.

It was still early, and the major crowds had not yet arrived. He helped Jaime climb onto one of the carousel horses. Reilly didn't need help, and Josh and Sassy sat in one of the carriages. As he sat down, he slid over to her side and took her hand.

Sassy felt a bit uneasy because she had not held hands with anyone since Kevin, but she thought it was a delightful feeling.

As the carousel began to move, Josh watched Jaime ahead of them. She turned and had a huge smile. Reilly sat stoically on the horse beside Jaime. Josh then turned to Sassy, and she also had a big smile.

They left the carousel and went to the Ferris wheel. Each car held two people, so Josh rode with Jaime, and Sassy rode with Reilly. For the next several hours, they went from ride to ride, laughing like Sassy had never laughed before. They had popcorn, cotton candy, and gallons of soft drinks. They saw a real dog and pony show, and later the show ponies were available for rides. When Sassy got tired from the walking, Josh rented a wheelchair and pushed her around. He said he didn't want to rent an electric cart because he wanted to push Sassy. He insisted it wasn't the money, he just wanted to push her. By the end of the day, they were all tired, full of junk food, and ready to go home.

After taking Jaime and Reilly home, he took Sassy back to her place and asked if he could come in for a few minutes. As they got inside, he sat down in the breakroom chair. "I haven't had so much fun in a long time."

"I haven't either. Thank you so much, Josh. It was a wonderful day. I may skip church tomorrow. I'm so tired from today."

"You'd better not skip church. I haven't been in months, but I should start going again. What time does church start?" he said as he got up and reached for her hand.

She took his, "Church starts at 10 AM."

"Great. I'll be by here to pick you up at 9:30." He leaned into her and gave her a gentle kiss. His lips were soft and moist, and he didn't press against hers firmly. It was a simple, friendly kiss. Her heart skipped a beat.

He backed off. He liked her. She was nice, fun, intelligent, and totally honest. He hoped to spend a lot of time with her in the coming weeks.

CHAPTER TWENTY-ONE

Millicent hung up the phone. "Detective Halligan isn't working on the case at all now. Since he has someone he thinks is guilty, he's moved on to other cases, like a stolen car and a home invasion. Finding a thief or burglar is now more important than finding a real killer."

"I thought that was the case. That's a good thing," Darcy added.

"Why is not working on the case a good thing?"

"Because we aren't getting in each other's way. We can just do our thing and won't be running into Halligan. Let's go back and talk to Susan Baxter again. We know she's not completely on the level."

They got to Susan's apartment a few minutes before lunch and knocked on her door.

They heard her voice through the video doorbell attached to the door frame.

"Hi there, Susan. It's Millicent Cooper. I'd like to speak with you about some of your art."

"Hold on, Millie, I'll be there in a minute."

Millie turned away from the camera and softly whispered to Darcy, "Follow my lead."

Darcy didn't reply, but Millie knew she would do as she instructed.

After several minutes, the door opened, and Susan sat in her wheelchair, backed it up and to the side. "Good morning, Millie. How are you? And you are doing well too, Darby?"

"Darcy," Darcy corrected her. "I'm doing well. Millie insisted I come along. I'm not an art person, but I do like some of your pieces."

Millie glided through the doorway. "Yes, Dee does like art. She raved about the Claiborne you have. We were hoping you would consider selling it."

"I don't know. I like it also, but we can talk. Everything has a price, you know."

Millie gave her an evil smile. "Yes, I know, and I was hoping you could tell us more about it. More about the art piece, I mean, and maybe we can arrive at a price?"

Susan wheeled into her living area and looked around. "Which one do you like, Darcy?"

Millie quickly pointed to the picture on the back wall. "She said she liked that one. What did you say about it, Dee?"

Darcy knew why Millie had pointed out that particular picture. She had no idea which one was the Claiborne. Millie knew. "I said it kind of grabbed me. I can't really say why. It just stands out. That's all."

Millie walked over to it, stood and stared. It was an abstract style, with slight three-dimensional paint strokes and depth. She raised her arm and began to trace the paint lines in the air. "Now that I look closer, I see it too. The bold colors give the viewer a feeling of joy and happiness, then as the paint goes down, it gets darker into a sad or depressed attitude."

Susan wheeled over to her. "As long as I've had that painting. I never saw it! But I see it now."

Millie quickly looked down at her. "It all depends on how you view it. If you look from top to bottom, you view it as joy descending into despair. I could say it's a bit like you. That chair now restricts you, though you were once young and full of life. A person who has lost a loved one could get the same feeling. Now, if you look at it from the bottom to the top, you see joy arising from despair. That same person after time, finds a new lover, and once again flies into happiness."

"You're very insightful, Millie. What do you see as you view it from left to right?"

"That's a simple one. Life has ups and downs. The next interesting thing is the artist didn't use a brush. He used a small paint spatula. That gives it a three-dimensional feel. Life is full of peaks and valleys, and we can't see them until we get close, or we must live it to understand it, Susan."

Darcy squinted her eyes. "All I see is some smeared blobs of pretty colors on a large canvas."

Millie turned, furrowed her eyes at Darcy, with a grimaced expression. She immediately looked down at Susan. Susan was still looking at the painting, tilting her head from side to side.

Darcy instantly knew Millie had disapproved of her opinion of the painting. "I just thought it was pretty, but now that you've explained it, I see exactly what you are talking about. It's a palette of life, in different colors."

Millie looked relieved at Darcy's response. She smiled at Darcy and looked back at the painting. "What are you willing to take for it, Susan?"

Susan pulled her chair backwards and looked at the painting from a few feet back. "I don't know. I never really thought of selling it."

"Give me a few days to think about it. Claiborne is an up-and-coming abstract artist, you know."

"True, but he's only up and coming in this area. That may not spread any farther than the city limits, and then only within the abstract art appreciators. He's not a Picasso or a Paul Cezanne."

Susan leaned back in her wheelchair. "We never know who is an artist in his or her cocoon. He may shed his caterpillar and become an international celebrity, Millie."

"The chances of winning the Powerball lottery are about the same as that happening."

"Maybe so, but people win the lottery even when the chances of winning are very low. How about 10K?"

"Sorry, but that is a bit high for a little-known artist," answered Millie.

"An up-and-coming artist."

"Maybe. When he 'comes up' a lot more, we can talk business. Anyway, that one is the one that Dee is interested in. I personally prefer traditional art. I like the Grant," Millie stated.

Susan mused, "Ah, the Lionel Grant. You like the Barn he painted. That is a No. 5 print."

Millie moved across the room to stand in front of the painting. "Yes. You told us last time we were here. You said that there are only 10 copies of the original?"

"Correct. I had the No. 5 and No. 8 of it, but I sold the 8." Susan pushed her chair over beside Millie. "To an astute collector, I might add."

"And what did he give you for it?"

"Well, I don't normally kiss and tell, but he gave me 8K for it."

Millie paused for a moment. "I see. Eight for an eight. Then you might sell me the No. 5 for 5K?"

Susan laughed haughtily. "Surely you jest. Now, if you're truly interested in my collection, let's talk seriously. Make me an offer."

Millie thought for a moment. "I'll go two thousand."

"Not a cent less than eight thousand. And since I sold the No. 8 for eight thousand, 8 is a deal. It is a Lionel Grant!"

It was Millie's turn to laugh. "I don't doubt what you paid for it, but I also know what it's worth. I buy nothing I don't make money on at the time of sale. I can have it sold for 6k within the week."

"So, you are a broker!" countered Susan.

"No, but like you, I sell my own pieces, and I'll not wait for ten years for it to appreciate in value. I have a network of buyers already. Do you?"

"Well, I, um..."

"If you could sell it for 8, it wouldn't be here on your wall. I'll give you three thousand for it, if you can supply certified papers for it," Millie said, staring directly down into Susan's deep blue eyes. "Come on, Dee. Let's go. Mrs. Baxter doesn't know enough about her paintings to know their true value."

As they headed to the door, Millie turned back to Susan, who was trying to keep up by wheeling her chair. "I'm sorry. I didn't mean to insult you. I just got carried away. Were you and Kevin Daniels working on your art trading together?"

Taken aback by the sudden change in topic, Susan's mouth dropped open and she stammered for a few seconds. "Yes. Kind of. Why do you ask that question?"

"No reason. I was just curious. Think about what we discussed and let me know. You can also make me a counteroffer on both paintings."

She reached down and gave her a business card. "I'm sure we can come to a reasonable deal. You have Darcy's number. This is my card. Call me, and we can talk more."

They walked out and down the stairs and got into Millie's Lamborghini. Darcy breathed a sigh of relief. "What in the world was all that about?"

Millie started the car and revved the engine a couple of times before putting it into gear. "She admitted that Kevin and she were working together. I deliberately hit her with that one. She wasn't expecting it. That's why she answered me. We need to check his and her bank account deposits. Next, if she's dealing with counterfeit paintings, it'll take her a few days to get the papers and the counterfeit painting. She'll swap the paintings with the ones on her walls and invite us over to pick them up, and she'll want payment in cash. I mean real American greenback dollars."

"Where did you learn all this stuff, Millie?"

"Ask me no questions, I'll tell you no lies. Now let's go see that attorney."

Back in Bridgeton, they pulled up at the law offices of Lawrence and Riggles. Inside they saw a cute little lady behind the main desk. "How can I help you?" she asked.

"We'd like to see Mr. Riggles," smiled Darcy.

"I'm sorry. He isn't in right now. He won't be back until late this afternoon," said the young lady.

"Is Mr. Lawrence available?" Asked Darcy.

"I'll check for you." She pressed a button and asked if Mr. Lawrence was free to see a client.

After the brief introductions, Darcy and Millicent sat in front of Mr. Lawrence.

"Now, ladies. How may I help you?"

"We're delving into the death of Kevin Samson. We were hoping you could answer just some general questions, and we'll be on our way," Darcy stated.

"I'll do what I can, but he was our researcher. I didn't use him much. Most of his work was for Jason, not me," the older gentleman stated.

"I understand," said Darcy. "We would like to clear up a few things. In our work, we hear a lot of rumors, most of which are false. We want to clear up some things. You know. Get the story straight."

He shook his head. "Okay, what rumors have you heard?"

Darcy adjusted herself and asked, "Our researchers say he took money from your clients' accounts, and your firm had to fix the problem?"

"I heard nothing about that. I don't even know how something like that would get out. We had no financial losses that we had to cover. Where did you hear that?" he asked.

"We have some researchers of our own. You see, Mr. Samson was killed, and we're trying to get all the records straight and turn them over to the district attorney. Our researchers didn't give us any names. Just the information. We have found several rumors that turned out not to be true. How about the affair that Mr. Samson was having with your secretary and Mr. Riggles' wife?"

"That one was true, I'm afraid. I don't have details, but we had to let him go because of it. We need to maintain integrity in our firm or the public will lose confidence in us and our services."

Darcy made notes in a small notebook. "We also heard that he got the secretary and Mrs. Riggles pregnant. Is that true?"

"I really shouldn't comment on that."

"I fully understand. We are just trying to clear up rumors. If we don't know the truth, we can't delete them from our files," Darcy added as she wrote.

"Yes, they both became pregnant, but I can't verify if Samson was the father. I can say that shortly after that, Mrs. Riggles committed suicide."

"Was that before or after their divorce?"

"After."

Darcy paused in her writing. "The autopsy report originally showed the cause of death of Mrs. Riggles was asphyxiation. She was strangled. Later, someone changed that to suicide. Can you verify that?"

"Look," he said, "I think I have given out more information than I should have. I can't say anymore."

"You have been very helpful, sir. We can use your clarification to correct our files before we turn them over to the DA," Darcy said, rising from her chair. She and Millicent shook his hand and left.

In the car, Millicent said, "Well, that was a waste of our time."

"Yep." She leaned back in her seat as Millicent drove them back to her home.

As they each dropped into a chair, Darcy leaned her head back in the chair. "I've got a screaming headache. Do you have a compress to put on my forehead?"

"Of course. I'll get it for you," she said, heading for the freezer. She grabbed an ice pack and wrapped it up in a towel, then passed it to Darcy.

Millicent sat down and began cross-referencing the information they had gotten.

CHAPTER TWENTY-TWO

The next morning, Darcy was sitting at her desk going over some balance and profit-and-loss statements when the intercom buzzed. "Yes, Monica?"

"A Mr. Gavin is on line one. He's with TOCO."

Darcy didn't know a Mr. Gavin and wondered what he was selling. "Hello, Mr. Gavin. How can I help you?"

"Mrs. Bower. I'm here to help a friend of yours. I'm calling regarding Sassafras Magill. I hope you have a few minutes to let me explain."

"I have a few minutes before my morning meeting. Please be brief, Sir." She sat back in her chair, with expectations of a sales pitch. She wasn't prepared for what he had to say.

After the phone call an hour later, the door burst open at Sassy's place when Darcy walked in and called her. "Sassy! Where are you? Is she in the back room, Jaime?"

Jaime nodded with a blank stare.

Darcy walked through the doorway and sat down beside Sassy. "We need to talk now!"

"Why? What's wrong?" asked Sassy.

"Nothing, but we need to talk. This afternoon, I will have some papers for you to sign at my office."

"What's going on, Darcy?" she asked, opening another case of oil to put onto a shelf in the front room.

"I got a call from a man in Texas. He wants to install a diesel pump in front of the store next to the gas pumps. He's willing to open a credit account for future gas and diesel deliveries."

"But I can't… I can't afford that. I hope you said no," said Sassy.

"I called our attorney and had the man and the company checked out. They're legitimate. It is a gas company in Houston, Texas. You already have a mortgage for the bond amount, but they agreed to take a second mortgage on the store and loan you the money at prime rate. You have six months to make your first payment on the pump installation loan. All you pay for at this time is the gas and diesel you buy, and you have 45 days to make each payment."

"How did you do that?" Sassy asked.

"I didn't. They called me. They heard about it from someone here in Bridgeton who believes you are being railroaded."

"But doesn't it take months to get city council approval, and building permits and stuff?"

"Apparently they have enough clout that they'll have permits by week's end. And construction will begin next Monday. One last thing. They are willing to pay all legal fees for your defense."

"Why would they do that?" Sassy looked confused.

"I guess someone believes you are innocent, and they're doing it to protect their investment in you. They want you out of jail to run the store," Darcy answered.

"I don't know what to say," Sassy stammered.

"Just be at my office at 5:00 PM. They already did the papers on their end and are emailing them to me. Our corporate lawyers are in-house, so they'll be there to read over everything on the real estate and construction stuff. Your defense lawyer will be there too."

"Darcy, you're wonderful." She reached out and hugged Darcy.

"I didn't really do anything but call our lawyers to verify everything. I've got to go now, but be at my office on time."

On the following Monday morning, Darcy and Sassafras were standing at the front of the store while trucks unloaded heavy equipment. First on the list of things to do was dig a hole for the underground diesel fuel tank. Another crew of men was unloading a pump and getting ready to set it beside the gasoline pumps.

"Wow. This is all happening so fast. I don't know how they got everything ready so quickly," said Sassy.

"I don't know either. I called my brother Mickey Ray. Even he doesn't know how they put it through. It takes us months of planning and city council meetings to get a project started," said Darcy in wonder.

Charlie, the cab driver, stopped and congratulated Sassy on the new pumps. "How long will it take before you can reopen?" he asked.

"It should be done in a few days, Charlie."

"That's great. It'll really help your business and raise your profit line," he said as he watched the men work.

"Yes. As I told you earlier, Darcy said she would send all their gas vehicles to fill up here. Now they can send their diesel ones too. It's a real help to me."

Josh also stopped by after making his morning deliveries. "They have really made progress in just a few hours. How long did they say it would take?"

Sassy smiled. "The supervisor said, if everything goes smoothly, it'll take three days. They will dig the holes today, install the new tanks tomorrow and run all the fuel lines. Then later tomorrow afternoon, the electrician will wire everything. The following day, it'll be paved over with quick-set concrete. By week's end, we can reopen the store for business."

"Who's doing this for you?" Josh asked.

"I have no clue. I signed papers from someone in Texas. They took care of everything. If I'm cleared of all criminal charges, I will pay it back. If I am convicted, they'll take the store. I guess that's fair. I can't run it from prison."

Josh put an arm around her and pulled her close. "You'll be cleared. I just feel it."

She leaned her head against his shoulder. "I hope you're right."

"Let's go out for dinner tonight. The store is closed, so you have some time off. My treat. If you don't mind riding in my junk heap car!"

"I don't mind at all. Since you're treating, where are we going?"

He thought for a moment. "I don't know. How about seafood?"

"That would be great, but right now, your work hours are being cut short, and we are both on a tight budget," she laughed.

"We can splurge tonight, then when the store opens again, we'll work hard and make it up."

"Are you sure? I can pay my part. It'll be easier on you," she suggested.

"Nope, tonight is for you," insisted Josh. "Maybe later when business picks up, you can pay. That is if you want to," he pulled her close, and she leaned on his shoulder again. She felt warm and comfortable with him. She hoped he was for real.

At dinner that night, she ordered a basic fish dinner. Even though he said she could order anything she wanted, she knew he was also on a budget, and she didn't want to take advantage of his generosity. Knowing how she was, he ordered a similar meal, so she wouldn't feel self-conscious of him paying for their meals. When he dropped her off, he opened the door and helped her get out.

When she opened the door to her place, he stepped inside ahead of her. He turned and pulled her to his chest and placed his lips against hers. At first, she slightly resisted, then as his warm body melted against hers, she gave in and returned the passionate act. Her heart sped up with the passion she was feeling.

As she was pressed against him, he also felt his heart beating in time with hers. Their hearts beat as one. As they kissed again, she began to shake. He slowly pushed away.

He raised his head but still looked into her eyes. "I.. um... have to go now."

"Can you stay for just a few more minutes, Josh?"

"I can't. I have to go while I still have the discipline to leave," he croaked. He turned and walked out of the door, closing it silently and gently behind him.

She was standing inside, still shaking from their kiss. What was she feeling? Was she falling in love with him? She thought she had loved Kevin, but his kisses were never like Josh's. She had never quite felt like this before. She watched him through the plate-glass window of the store. He got to his car and stopped, then looked back and blew her a kiss.

Even at that distance, she felt her heart skip another beat at this small action on his part. He got into his car and drove off. She was all alone again, but this time she was happy.

With her disability, it was usually a real journey just to hold on to the handrail and pull herself up the stairs. Tonight, she barely remembered that slow walk. She felt as though she was gliding up to her bedroom. She fell asleep and rested better than she had slept in weeks.

The construction was completed on time as promised, and Josh helped Sassy, Jaime and Reilly put up some fresh signs in front of the store announcing their new diesel pump. Diesel and gasoline vehicles from the Christianson company were the first ones in line when they opened that day. It was a banner day for Sassy and her store. Josh had taken the day off from his delivery job to help with the increased business.

At the end of the day, when they closed the doors, Josh took out a bottle of Champagne, and they toasted the new store opening. Since Reilly and Jaime were over twenty-one, he gave them each just a sip of Champagne so they could feel a part of the celebration. Reilly accepted a handshake from Josh, and Jaime blushed when Josh gave her a kiss on the cheek. It was another good day for Sassy and her staff. That night, Sassafras Magill went to sleep tired but happy.

CHAPTER TWENTY-THREE

Millicent put the papers down on the table. "I think I've found a connection between Susan's foreign accounts and Kevin's. The ones they both have in the UK that are with the same bank have deposits on the same day almost at the same time. See here?" she said, holding a piece of paper. It had a photograph with a line connecting the US to the Bank of London.

"I see, but what does that tell us?"

"Look at the amounts of deposits and transfers. At first, his are small and at the same time as Susan's deposits. The last few are direct transfers from her accounts to his and in sizeable sums. Then all activity stops. That was around the time he was killed. Those transfers give Susan a motive to kill Kevin. He was stealing her money through the transfers. I didn't see these accounts. You have to trace each one like a ball of string. It goes from one bank to another, and then to another. It gets almost confusing. That's why I didn't see it. So far, I've seen he has a total of four point six million in combined accounts around the world."

Darcy sat up. "He wasn't nearly as naïve as we thought he was. He really had Susan Baxter fooled."

"I'll spend a bit more time on her art trading." Millie blew out a deep breath and imitated Darcy's pose at looking at the ceiling when she's thinking.

They both sat on the couch, staring at the ceiling. "Why do you look at the ceiling like this?" asked Millicent.

"I originally got it from Mickey Ray. I asked him the same thing. He said it's best when you're in a recliner. It helps you clear your mind.

When you look around at the walls, and even out windows, you see things. Ceilings are blank. Nothing distracts your thoughts."

They both sat and thought in silence. Finally, Darcy spoke up. "We put Sasan Baxter at the top of the suspect list. Who's next?"

"I think we should look at Riggles' accounts. While you were napping, I also ran his transfers and didn't get any significant connections. But I got a withdrawal around the time of his wife's death. That one was for ten thousand dollars cash. It doesn't show up with a corresponding deposit anywhere on this entire page," stated Millicent.

"It could have been a hitman," said Darcy. "Yes. That's the downside of staring at a ceiling. You tend to fall asleep."

"Yep. A hitman. That was exactly my thoughts. If he had had her killed, he could also have had Kevin killed."

"I don't think so. Why kill her immediately and wait two years to kill Kevin?"

"That leaves Hollis," mused Millicent.

"We need to check him out too, but he doesn't fit the profile. He's exceedingly rich but doesn't seem to care. We could go see him again and snoop around his finances a little more," yawned Darcy.

"Girl, you need to get more sleep."

"Let's go see Satchel Hollis again. Tomorrow."

The next morning, she was knocking on Millicent's door. Millie answered the door with a yawn. "Hey, girl, why are you so early?"

"It's almost nine thirty. I've been by the office, had a short meeting, had breakfast and now I'm here. What have you been doing?"

"More bank account searches and connections."

"And what did you find?"

"I found several things. One is Satchel Hollis made a withdrawal of twenty thousand dollars one week before Kevin was killed. Second, Gary Grayson, had a ten thousand dollar deposit in another bank. It does not have his wife on the account. That raises some real flags."

"Why didn't we see that before now?"

Millie started making a cup of instant coffee. "I don't know. Your source didn't find it either. Don't blame me, Dee! You want a cup?"

"Instant coffee? Oh, gosh, no. That stuff tastes nasty."

"Yes, but my taste buds aren't awake yet," she said as she stirred the cup of brown liquid. "So, what now?"

"I'm going to make a real cup of coffee."

"Help yourself. By the time that pot's ready, I'll be awake enough for a cup. So, what now?"

"All of them look bad, but we don't have a shred of evidence against any of them. Have you looked at the others? How about Tracy Larson? She was the secretary at Lawrence and Riggles," Darcy said as she tapped the side of the coffee maker.

"I know. One person at a time, Dee. I'll get to Mrs. Larson as soon as I can. I can hack her bank account, but I can't see her entire financial situation. Maybe your source can do that?"

"You mean Valerie? Yes, she can see everything that's online. I'll get her to run it down for us." Darcy made a call and within minutes, her printer was spitting out Tracy Larson's bank statements.

Millie took a quick look and announced, "Tracy has a little over one hundred thousand in the bank. She's right. That won't last but a few years. She'll have to go back to work, and she's got a toddler to raise. That's a motive for her to have killed Samson. He left her high and dry."

Darcy took a deep breath and sighed. "Sometimes I wish we had never gotten involved with this stuff."

"You can't say that, because you're more invested in this case than I am. You care. Don't deny it, Dee."

"Yeah. You're right. Look at all these suspects. We have motives for everyone, but no connecting evidence. I can't fix the world, Millie. What if we don't find the killer and clear Sassy's name? She goes to prison for something she didn't do. The police aren't even trying. They don't care about finding the actual killer. All they care about is making a conviction, so they look good. It'll look good on the DA's record." She folded her arms on the countertop and laid her head on them. "I'm tired. I worry more about Sassafras than I do about my family. I get to the office early, then spend the day with you tracking down leads. Then back to the office to catch up on work, I get home late and spend a few minutes with the kids. I go to their school functions and have very little time for my husband."

"You're tired. I get it. We'll find Kevin's killer, and it'll all be worth it. I promise. At least you have a husband and family. All I have is this big house, and lots of money. Money doesn't keep me warm at night. Why do you think I'm up half the night watching old movies? And now I have something to do that is really worthwhile."

Darcy raised her head. "And what's that?"

"Helping you with this case, silly. Now, get up and help me sort this stuff out. You can catch up on your sleep when we solve this case. You're feeling sorry for yourself right now. Get over it, girlfriend!"

Darcy sat up, yawned and said, "We need to interview Satchell Hollis again."

Millie jumped up and grabbed her purse. "I agree, so let's go!"

Darcy slowly got off the stool at the counter and grabbed her purse as well.

When they pulled into Satchel Hollis's driveway, he was once again standing in the doorway of his home. He smiled and raised a glass of some kind of drink.

"Hello, ladies. I'm glad to see you again!" he called to them as they got out of the car.

"How do you do that, Satchel?" Millie called back.

"I have a gift. Come on in, ladies."

As they followed him in, they looked around the estate. They saw several men working on the shrubs and grounds. All were foreign, mostly of Mexican or Latin descent, which made Dee and Millie wonder about their work status. They went through the house again, and back to the pool area, where his wife Doris was also sipping on a fruity-looking drink.

Darcy sat down in the chair beside Doris. "How are you doing?"

"I'm doing well, and how are both of you?"

Millie also sat. "We are doing well also."

"What can I do for you ladies this beautiful morning?" asked Satchel as he sat beside Doris.

"We were wondering where you get your help. We saw all the people working on your yard and grounds, and Hazel, your housekeeper."

Satchel suddenly got serious. "I see. You get right down to business. You aren't really here to find out where I get my domestic help. There are employment agencies in Bridgeton you can call. Last time you were here, you asked about Kevin Samson. Now you are asking for my help."

Darcy looked him straight in the eyes. "That's true, but we need help, and it's well known that sometimes foreign help are better workers than people that live here. Also, they work a lot cheaper than local help."

"I looked you up, Darcy Jean Christianson Bower. Tell me what you really want? I have a gut feeling you aren't here to find additional employees. Why are you really here?"

Darcy moved uncomfortably in her seat, and again looked directly into Satchel's piercing blue eyes, then turned slightly to Doris, who was also boring her eyes into her.

"You looked me up. What did you find, Satchel?"

"You are one of the principal officers of the Christianson Company, along with your brother, Mickey Ray. You are married to James Bower, an actual war hero. You don't normally hire foreign help."

Millie had said nothing so far. "We want to know where you get your help, Satchel."

He looked at her and gave her a sly smile, then politely answered. "I don't think that's any of your business."

"Come on, Satchel. If you've done nothing wrong, then why don't you tell us?" Millie answered just as politely.

"I admit nothing illegal, but I'm not answering that question. I treated each of you with respect and answered your questions honestly about Kevin Samson. Now you come back and pry into my personal business. I resent that, ladies."

Darcy spoke up again. "I understand your position, sir. We also did some background checks on you too. There is no record with the National Immigration Service of your filing any papers of support or sponsorship of any foreign people. We can only deduce that the people we see working here are all illegal workers."

"What do you plan to do about it?"

"Absolutely nothing," said Millie.

"Then I ask you again, why are you here?" asked Satchel.

"We want to know everything you know about Kevin Samson," answered Darcy.

"I told you all I know."

"You didn't know he was a con man? I find that difficult to believe," Millie asked.

He got up from his seat and motioned for Darcy and Millicent to do the same. "I do now. Listen, ladies, you could have discussed all of this over the phone. I have a lot of things going on, and as you already know, I won the lottery, and because of that, I have con men, cheats, and scammers coming out of the woodwork. He is one that slipped through the cracks, so I just moved onward and didn't look back. Now, if you don't mind, I have some things I need to attend to. You are welcome to come back for a social visit. But not if you are here to harass me or get information to report me to the authorities for some made-up criminal activities."

As Millicent stood up, she remarked, "So, you are saying we can't report you to the authorities?"

"I can't tell you what you can and cannot do, but I highly advise you not to report anything you have heard or seen here. Good day, ladies. You may see yourselves out," he answered as he sat back down in his chair.

As they drove away in Millicent's Lamborghini, she commented, "Well, that was another waste of time."

Darcy stared out the windshield. "He's hiding something. I bet he's running a human trafficking operation. We can come back to him again sometime. If Kevin had known what Satchel was doing, he could have blackmailed him, and Hollis killed him for it."

"He could have done a lot of things, but we have no evidence. For now, that's only conjecture," answered Millie.

"Yeah. I guess so," Darcy said as she closed her eyes in thought.

Back at Millie's home, they examined the data collected by Monica, Millicent, and Valerie.

Darcy suddenly looked up from the stack of papers in front of her. "We need to go back, and check the GPS on the cars of every one of the suspects and the GPS of their phones."

"And how do we do that?" asked Millicent.

"I'll call Valerie. She can get that information for us. You go back and pull up the bank statements from everyone around the time of Kevin's death. We can compare all of them. I'll have her pull up every vehicle in the area around the time Kevin was killed."

Darcy made a call to Valerie and then put her on speakerphone. "Good morning, Darcy Jean. How are you today?"

"I'm fine, Valerie, and how are you today?"

"I'm doing fine. You are so polite. Much more polite than your husband, James," Valerie answered.

Darcy rolled her eyes at Millicent and continued talking to Valerie. "Yes, I know, but I hope you'll forgive him. He's just preoccupied most of the time. You know. All business."

"I realize that, but I will forgive him because you are the sister of my one true love, Mickey Ray."

Millicent gave Darcy a questioning look. Darcy gave her another eye roll. "I have a favor to ask of you, Val."

"I have locked onto your location. May I access Ms. Cooper's computer, and will you put me on the main monitor so we can see each other?"

Millie nodded her head, yes.

"Sure, Val. She has a large-screen monitor on her wall. She'll turn that on, so we can talk from there."

Millicent clicked a few keys on the keyboard of her laptop on the kitchen counter, and the large wall monitor came alive.

On the screen was a beautiful woman sitting at a small table sipping a tropical fruity drink at a beach bar. In the background, the sun was shining, and beautiful bikini-clad women were playing volleyball. The waves were lapping at the shoreline, with people running in and out of the water. In the distance, a few people were surfing a curl.

Millicent looked at the screen in wonder. "Where are you?"

"I'm in your computer, Millicent."

Millicent looked from the screen to Darcy in astonishment. "Who is she?"

Darcy laughed. "She's an AI computer program. The image she has put up for us isn't real. Neither is she. That is her own generated image."

"OMG. It is gorgeous. I thought it was real."

"Thank you, Millicent. You are also beautiful. But please refer to me as 'she', not 'it'. And I am real, just as you are real. You are flesh and blood. I am a computer program, but I'm real."

Millicent again looked at Darcy. "Is 'it' — I mean 'she' — for real?"

"Yes, sort of. It's hard to explain. We'll talk about it later. For now, just treat her as you would any other person."

Valerie made a sound as though she was clearing her throat. "What may I do for you, Dee? While you were both discussing me, I ran a thorough background check on Millicent Cooper. My conclusion is that she is trustworthy. You may tell her about me, if you choose to do so."

"So, I'm trustworthy, you say?" mocked Millicent.

Darcy said to Millie, "Don't get into an argument with her now, Millie. She is only trying to protect me. As she gets to know you as I know you, she can be very helpful, but I must warn you, Valerie can be stubborn and petty. She picks up on voice tonality quickly and does not deal well with sarcasm. Okay?"

Millie sat down on the bar stool at the counter with a frown. "Okay."

"Thank you, Millie. Now, Val, we need some more information."

"What do you need from me? Is this a 'for your eyes only' Darcy Jean?"

"No. You can share it with Millie as well. Just send it to her printer, please," Darcy continued, requesting information.

Valerie AI made a sound like a human "hmmm" then said it would be faster if she assigned it to some assistants in her network. She also added that she would answer by sending the reports to the printer. Valerie smiled and asked, "Would you like me to remain online in case you have other requests?"

"That will be all, Valerie, and thank you for your help."

"You are welcome, but I will remain on standby." Then the screen went blank.

"Wow, she's really cool, Dee. But I don't know whether I like her or not."

Suddenly, a voice came over the speaker. "When you get to know me, you will love me. I'm a very lovable person."

Millie looked around the room. "Was that her listening to us?"

Darcy called out, "Val. Do not eavesdrop on our conversation. You may only listen and respond to a specific call to you! Do you understand?"

"I understand," said the voice.

"Whoa, that's so cool," Millie said. "How long will it take her to do that? What did she mean by her assistant?"

"I don't completely understand, but she has somehow put together an extensive computer network. She'll assign different computers to do different tasks and then compile the results and send them to your printer."

"I don't get it."

Darcy took a deep breath. "Me neither."

CHAPTER TWENTY-FOUR

Charlie had filled up his cab and walked into Sassy's Place to pay for the purchase. In one corner was Josh putting items on the higher shelves, and Sassafras putting things on the lower shelves.

"Hello, Sassy. How are things going since you installed the new pumps?" he asked as he walked to the register.

"They're going great, Charlie. How are things going for you?"

"Okay, I guess. I'm getting adequate fares. At least enough to pay my bills, so I can't complain. You haven't called me for a ride for a couple of weeks now."

"Yeah. Josh takes me to the store to pick up things I can't get delivered here."

"You know, I give you a discount on my fares," he said, laying cash on the counter as Josh rang up the gas purchase.

"I know, but we are trying to cut costs until I get back on my feet, and someone drops this murder charge. I really hope that Darcy Bower and her partner find the killer before my trial."

"They may not find Kevin's killer, but I hope they get the charges against you dropped."

"Me too," Sassy sighed.

"Keep your chin up, Sassafras. I'm sure the police don't have enough evidence against you to convict you," he said, walking out the door.

Josh closed the register. "He seems like a nice guy. How long have you known him?"

"We went to school together. Sometimes the kids would laugh and make fun of me. He looked out for me when we were kids. He's a good friend."

Millie and Darcy were looking at the GPS printouts of all vehicles and cell phones in the area where Kevin was killed. There were quite a few, and they checked the numbers and names.

Darcy sat back in the chair. "My eyes are beginning to cross from all this. I need some sleep. The kids have barely seen me for days. I'm going home. We can pick this up tomorrow, Millie."

"Got it. I'll keep cross-referencing these names and numbers until you get back in the morning. Say 'hi' to the kids and James for me."

"Yep," she said, walking out the door.

At the store, Sassy and Josh were wrapping it up for the day. "OMG, Josh, we had a banner day! The highest dollar sales I've ever had."

Josh smiled at her. He put the last item on the shelf, and walked over to her, and took her in his arms. "Stop work now. We gotta talk. We can finish this tomorrow."

She felt so warm and safe in his arms. She placed her head on his chest and sighed. "I wish all this would go away. Things are getting better and worse at the same time. I'm so afraid I might go to prison for something I didn't do."

He gently stroked her hair. "Let's go back into the back room, sit down and talk." He backed away, took her hand, and together they walked to the back room. When they sat down on the couch in the corner, he just looked into her eyes. She was tearing up.

She looked back at him with a puzzled expression on her face. "What? Oh, no ... You're going to break up with me! What did I do?"

He sat silently, letting her vent to him. Finally, he reached out and put his finger on her lips. "Shh... I'm not breaking up with you. I love you..."

Her mouth dropped open. "But..."

Again, he pressed a finger to her lips. Softly. Gently. Almost a whisper, he said, "Sassafras Magill. I love you. I want you to be my wife!"

"You what?"

"Silly girl. I'm trying to propose to you."

Tears flooded down her face. "I... I don't know what to say."

"Say one word. Say yes."

With tears running down her cheeks, she croaked, "Yes."

"Now, I need to say one more thing." He whispered as he leaned over and gently kissed her on the lips. He felt her warm tears. He stroked her face and repeated the kiss.

"What?" she asked.

"Say that you love me too, my dear," he whispered into her ear.

"Yes. Yes. A thousand times yes," she continued crying, now tears of joy.

As they leaned in with affection and kisses, they embraced. "What if I go to prison?" she asked.

He sat back and smiled again. "I have complete confidence in Darcy Christianson. She'll figure all this out. It'll be fine. Darcy recommended your attorney. I'm sure he is the best and he'll make sure you don't go to jail."

"But what if I do? As my husband, you'll incur all the debt of the new pumps, and the store. You don't want to be saddled with all that."

"As your husband, I'll take care of it. You'll be my wife, for better or worse. We'll get married as soon as possible. It'll take time to plan a wedding, but we can do it together."

"Oh, no. Not a big wedding. We can't afford that. Just a small one at the church my family attends," she said between sobs.

"Whatever you want. I'll live my life to make you happy. You'll be the most important person in my life," he said as he sat back and watched the tears continue to trickle down her face. "I never want to see tears of anything but happiness from now on, my love."

She wiped her face and gave him a tear-stained smile. "I love you so much."

"I've got to go now. I have to go home and call my parents and tell them I've found their newest family member. We're going to get married! I'll see you in the morning, and it'll be the best day I've ever had!" he said as he got up to leave. He could have sworn he saw her eyes sparkle as he'd never seen them before. He wanted so much to stay, but he had to leave while he could.

The following morning, Darcy got to Millicent's house, and the door was locked, so she had to knock. That was unusual, but soon the doorbell camera lit up and Millie's groggy voice called over the speaker. "Sorry, Dee. Use the hidden key to let yourself in. I'll be down in a few minutes." The intercom clicked silent again.

Darcy reached under the flowerpot near the front door. She had told Millie a dozen times not to hide a key under a flowerpot, a fake rock or over the top of the door trim, but she never listened. As she took the key and let herself in, she headed to be kitchen and started a pot of fresh coffee.

As the pot dripped the hot brown liquid into the carafe, Millie walked slowly into the room with her hands stretched with palms down like zombies did in the movies. "Coffee. I need coffee," she stated in a slow, eerie voice.

"You look horrible," said Darcy.

"I feel horrible. I was awake until three this morning sorting all this stuff out. I think I have solved it. I'll explain it to you. Then we need to head to the police station to give them what we have so they can make some arrests." She poured herself a cup of coffee and reached for the printouts.

Pointing a finger, she said, "Look at this number, and where it originated, and who it was to and from."

Darcy nodded her head as Millie continued pointing and connecting the lines from each number and caller.

"I don't know why the police didn't see this in the beginning," Millie said.

"Because they don't have the resources we have," answered Darcy. "Also, they may not use this in a courtroom. Since some of this stuff was obtained without proper warrants."

"True, but if they use it properly, maybe they can get a confession."

"We can give it to the police and let them see what they can do."

CHAPTER TWENTY-FIVE

Sassy heard the front door of the store close, and Josh called out. "Good morning. Where are you?"

"I'm back in the break room making some biscuits. Come on back," she answered.

Josh walked back and stood in front of a plate of ragged-looking, semi-soggy biscuits. "You baked these?" as he made a face.

"Of course not, silly. I got them out of the freezer and microwaved them. You know, I rarely cook," she laughed.

He took her hand and gently kissed it. "When we get married, I think cooking will be my job," he teased.

With a huge smile, she questioned, "Why do you need to wait until then? You can start cooking anytime."

"Maybe I'll do that. Hey, why don't we have Jaime and Reilly come back now that the store is in full operation?"

"I don't know. Now I have a payment to make on the diesel pump outside. We also have a wedding to plan."

"Hire a wedding planner."

"We don't have that kind of money. Besides, all we need is a small wedding, with a few friends and family."

"I called my parents' last night and told them the news. They were ecstatic. My mother wants her oldest son to have a nice wedding."

"It will be nice, but it doesn't have to be big or expensive. We'll have the wedding at my church, and the reception can be in the church's basement. They have a very nice reception hall just for that. When are we getting married?"

"As soon as we can get it set up. I want you for my own as soon as possible!"

They heard the front door close, and a voice called out, "Sassy, are you here? I came in to pay for my gas."

Josh walked into the front room of the store. "Good morning, Charlie. How are you this fine day?" he said as he approached Charlie behind the counter at the register area.

"I'm doing fine, Josh. Is Sassy down yet?"

"Sure, she's making coffee. We haven't set up the one out here yet. But I can get you a cup from back there. Want a cup?"

"Umm... No, I guess I've gotta get back out on the street. I have a couple of regulars who catch me almost every morning to take them to their offices. How is she holding up?"

"She's doing great. The murder case's resolution will relieve both of us," Josh said.

"Yeah, I guess it will. Good luck on that," Charlie said as he walked out the door.

As the day progressed, Josh watched the store while Sassy made calls and started work planning their wedding.

"Josh?" she called out as she cupped her hand over the phone. "Is the Saturday after next okay for the wedding? That is the soonest the reception room will be available at the church?"

"Sure, but why don't you call Luigi's for the reception room, and we can have a nice formal dinner for the guests? Right after the wedding," Josh replied.

"Honey, I don't think we can afford the room and dinner for a lot of people like that."

"We'll find a way to afford it. Just make sure the preacher is available."

"Okay. If you say so," she talked again into the phone. "Saturday after next in the evening is okay at Luigi's," she called again to Josh.

He nodded to her as he made change for a customer.

After hanging up the phone, she walked over to him. "I can't wait to be your wife, Josh."

"I can't wait to be your husband. How are your parents taking this whirlwind romance of ours?"

"Momma and Daddy are thrilled for us. Momma wants us to go shopping for a dress tomorrow. Can you handle the store?"

"Sure. And I have to tell you something."

"Okay, things should be a bit slow for a while. Let's sit down and talk." They pulled up two chairs at the end of the store counter and sat.

Josh took a deep breath. "Okay. First things first. My parents will be flying in on Wednesday, so Saturday will be good for the wedding. Next. I quit my job at the supply house. I gave Glenda notice last week. So, I can work here full time now."

"Oh, no. We can't afford it. Now, it'll take both our paychecks to pay the bills."

He leaned over and gave her a gently kiss. "From now on, I will take care of everything. No, you will never have another worry in your life. I also called Jaime and Reilly to come back to work here. We won't have to put in such long hours when we get married."

"That's a lot of financial burden you'll be taking on, Josh. Are you sure? You are or were just a delivery driver. Are you sure you can run the store business? I mean, I grew up here, and my parents showed me how it works." She patted his arm. "But that's okay. I'll work with you and show you how it's done. We'll be a team. I'll teach you the ropes of running this store," she smiled.

"I knew you'd be here to help me learn the process. We'll make this the biggest convenience store in all of Bridgeton. Now we still have some inventory to put on the shelves during this slow time," he said, getting up and heading to the stockroom.

CHAPTER TWENTY-SIX

Darcy and Millie sat in front of Detective Halligan. Darcy spread out printouts of cell phone calls and vehicle GPS data from Lakeside City Park on the night Kevin died.

When they spread out the sheets, Darcy let Millicent explain to the detective what had happened.

"If you see here, detective. This number corresponds to this name. It's his cell phone's GPS, also there is also the corresponding GPS on his vehicle. At the same time. The phone and vehicle stayed at the same location for thirty-two minutes. Then they departed and returned to the original address where they were both registered. We can even tell by this GPS and phone GPS that the other vehicle was here and waited for 45 minutes, then moved to the location where the body was found. Then moved away and left the area."

"How did you get these printouts, Ms. Cooper?"

"What's more important? Where I got it, or that we found Kevin Sampson's killer?"

"I asked you a question. I expect an answer."

"We expect you to arrest this killer and drop all charges against Sassafras Magill."

"Did you have a warrant to get this information? If this wasn't gotten legally, it won't be allowed in court. So, you don't have any usable evidence."

"Sassafras is innocent. You have to drop the charges!"

"You may leave my office until you bring me legal and acceptable evidence of another killer. Her trial will take place. Now, you may leave. I have other cases to work on."

"So, you don't care if she goes to prison?"

"I care that I have a killer, and I'll let a jury decide her guilt or innocence. That's not my job."

In the car, both ladies were fuming at the lackadaisical attitude of Detective Halligan. "He doesn't care one bit about getting the actual killer. He cares only about getting a conviction under his belt. It makes him look good as a cop!"

"What do you suggest we do now, Dee?"

"We get him to confess to killing Kevin," she said as she started the car. "We wait for him to get home and then confront him with the evidence we have."

As they drove to the house, Darcy called out to Valerie. When Valerie answered through the car radio, Millie looked at Darcy with genuine admiration, but didn't say a word. "Good morning, Darcy Jean. How may I help you?"

"Can you tap into the Bridgeton police station intercom system?"

There came a slightly mechanical laugh over the radio. "Of course. That is child's play for me."

"Alright, when we get there, I would like you to sync with my and Millie's phones. In case something happens to one, we will have the other as backup."

"It is done. I'm synced with both phones."

"Good, we don't need you at this time, but we'll give you a signal when we need it," Darcy said as she pulled onto the street where he lived. "You begin recording over the police station intercom and record when I say the code word, 'sync.'"

Valerie said, "Understood. On standby until the code word 'sync' is used."

They parked across the street and waited until he got home. Finally, Gary Grayson pulled his truck into the driveway, got out and headed for his front door. Darcy moved the car in front of the driveway, blocking his truck. Darcy and Millie got out and followed him to the door.

"Hello, ladies. To what do I owe this pleasure?"

Darcy stood at the bottom of the steps and looked up at Gary, who was putting his key into the door lock. "We need to talk to you and Karen."

"What about? Do you have the money that Kevin-what's-his name took from us?"

"Sorry, but no. Is Karen home?" Millie asked.

"I assume she is. Her car is there," he said, pointing to the small SUV parked in front of his truck. "She's probably cooking dinner."

He opened the door and called out, "Karen. I'm home. We have guests."

Karen walked into the living room with a large serving spoon in her hand. "Hello," she said with a questioning look.

"We won't be long. We just came by to tell you we know who killed Kevin Samson, or Daniels, as you knew him."

Karen dropped her spoon. "I don't understand," she said shakily.

"Sync," said Darcy loudly.

"Okay, I'll put the spoon in the sink. Let me get a rag to mop up the grease from the floor," Karen said.

Darcy smiled at herself. Only she and Millie knew what she was doing.

"Why don't we all sit until Karen comes back?" Darcy said as she and Millie sat on the couch. "Where are the kids?"

Karen came back and wiped the floor with a rag, placed it on the table behind her, and came back into the living room area. "They're at my mother's house. My parents are taking care of them for a few days."

"We want you to tell us about Kevin Samson," Millie said.

Karen cleared her throat and croaked, "I...um...don't know what you mean?"

"I think you do," added Darcy.

"Which one of you killed him?" said Millie.

Gary spoke up. "We don't know what you're talking about."

Karen got up. "I think it's time for you to leave!"

"We aren't leaving. The police will be here in a few minutes to arrest you for the murder of Kevin Samson, or as you knew him, Kevin Daniels."

"We did nothing. He stole our money," Karen said. "I wanted to meet him to force him to give us our money back, but he said he didn't have it. He said that Gary knew what he was getting into. When you invest money, there is always a chance of losing it. He told my stupid moron husband it was very little chance of that happening! We saved for five years to get that money. We need a bigger house!"

"Oh, pu-lease!" said Millie. "We know for a fact that you called Kevin and asked to meet him at the park on the night he died. You met him that night. After that, Gary joined you for about fifteen minutes. Then you left. Gary stayed for another ten minutes, and then he left too. You then joined again at an all-night diner for another hour before you came back home."

"You don't know that!" Gary said. "You can't prove anything you just said."

Darcy chimed in. "Yes. We can prove it. And we'll give the police our evidence, and you'll both go to jail."

"Wait," Gary said. "You don't understand. That was hard-earned money. I put in a lot of overtime for that money, and Kevin stole it from us. He was... he was an awful person!"

"I agree, but that didn't give you the right to kill him! You could have gone to a lawyer and sued him for the money."

"Sue him? Are you kidding? Lawyers cost money. We don't have the kind of money they said they'd charge. We went to one, and he told us we had to pay all filing fees up front and give him one third of the amount of the lawsuit. That was win or lose! He also said that even if we win the case, we may not collect the money. That's why he wanted his fee upfront," Gary stated.

"I'm sorry about that. Now, we need you to come with us to the police station and turn yourselves in," said Darcy calmly.

Karen turned to Gary. "I told you something bad would happen when you got involved with that shyster. I should have taken the kids and left you years ago!"

"What? You're the one who killed him with that rock you smashed him with!" he said back to her.

"I didn't mean to kill him. I picked it up only to scare him, you idiot!" she screamed.

"With a rock? You were going to scare him with a rock. You really are a dumb girl, Karen."

"At least I didn't bring a gun like you did, Gary!"

"Maybe I did, but it was for protection. I didn't shoot the guy. You are so stupid! I'm leaving and never coming back!" he screamed as he got up.

"Wait. Both of you! No one is going anywhere," called Darcy. "The police are on the way as we speak, Gary."

"No, they're not. You're bluffing," he said as he continued moving to the door.

"Don't call my bluff. I mean it. Besides, if you didn't kill Kevin, you have nothing to worry about. When we were here before, I saw the bandage Karen had on her wrist." She pointed to Karen's arm. "It's healed enough that she only needs a band-aid now. When we asked about the kids, she said that her parents were keeping them for a few days. The last time we were here, she said that her parents were dead." Darcy sat back on the couch.

Karen again spoke up. "It's none of your business where our kids are! And I didn't kill him. When I left, he was still alive. I didn't hit him that hard on the head with that stupid rock." Darcy looked at Gary for confirmation.

"It's true. When she left, he was still alive, but his head was bleeding. I tried to stop it, but I had nothing to wrap around it. I couldn't take off my shirt to use it as a bandage because I knew it could be traced back to me. There was blood everywhere. Karen cut herself on the edge of the rock she hit him with."

"Okay. I believe you. There were two samples of blood on the rock. One was Kevin, and the other was unidentified, which I'm sure will turn out to be Karen's blood."

Gary hung his head. "Oh god. This has been an absolute nightmare."

"Before the police get here, why don't you tell us your side?" suggested Millicent.

He started, "Well, when we found out Kevin's real name, I called him. He kept telling me that everything would work out. All I had to do was be patient. When Karen finally told me she knew all about what I had done, she called him and asked to talk and work something out.

"He said they could meet at the park at ten o'clock that night. Karen called and told me about the meeting, but I wanted to be there too. I was working late that night, but I took off early to meet both. When I got there, they were already in a heated argument. I tried to calm them down and talk rationally. He called her a slut and some other horrible names."

"He offered to pay everything back if I would sleep with him. I told him I would never sleep with a pig like him," Karen interjected. "I saw Gary pull in beside my car in the distance. We were down by the lake next at one of the benches that overlooked the water. We were both sitting on the bench when Gary pulled up..."

"When I parked," Gary interrupted Karen and continued with his story, "I saw them each get up. I didn't know what they were saying, but I could tell they were arguing.

"Suddenly he turned around and started to walk away. I saw Karen bend down and pick up a large stone that was used as a border stone on the path leading around the lake. She hit him with it, and he fell. She told me what happened, and I told her to leave. There was blood everywhere. He died a few minutes later. I couldn't do anything, so I left too."

Darcy shook her head in disgust. "You could have called 911, or moved him to your truck, and taken him to the hospital, but you didn't. Then you covered it up and denied the entire thing. Maybe he deserved what happened, but it wasn't up to either of you to be judge, jury and executioner." As Darcy was speaking, the police with sirens and flashing lights pulled up to the curb in front of the house.

Millie glared at both Karen and Gary. "I think your ride is here. We'll go out to greet them. Just sit and they'll soon be here to cuff you."

Millicent and Darcy got up and walked outside, spoke to the office in charge and left.

CHAPTER TWENTY-SEVEN

The wedding went smoothly at the little Baptist church in Bridgeton. Sassafras looked radiant in her mother's wedding dress, and Josh was in a rented tuxedo and looked very handsome.

The mothers of the bride and groom were crying tears of joy while both fathers looked on at the ceremony with great pride. After the ceremony, it was announced that a reception was being held at Luigi's Italian restaurant, and all were welcome to join the festivities.

When Darcy and her family arrived, Mickey and Millie were already there. Sassy and Josh were standing in the receiving line, shaking hands with everyone that came in. There was a combo band playing soft music in the far corner of the room. Decorations were hanging from the ceiling and on the tables.

"Oh, Darcy. Thank you so much. You literally saved my life. We're both so happy and appreciative of all you have done for us," said Sassafras, with tears in her eyes. Josh just smiled and thanked them.

Darcy saw Detective Halligan and walked over to him. "Well, Detective Halligan, I guess you are here to apologize to Sassy?"

"Nope. I was doing my job, so I don't have to apologize for that," he said with a smug smile.

"I beg to disagree with you. Millie and I did your job. You did nothing to find the actual killer."

He looked at the two of them. Again, his wry smile appeared. "You are absolutely correct. You see, where I come from, I was under pressure to get credible suspects. The district attorney was under pressure to get convictions. I didn't like that. I wanted the real criminals, not some numbers to make myself look good."

"So, you thought that Sassafras was a credible suspect?" asked Millie.

"Not for a minute. I checked her out. I never believed she was guilty, but my workload was high for a Podunk town like Bridgeton. Since I didn't have the time or resources to find the actual killer, I recruited the two of you."

"Wait. What? What do you mean, you recruited us! You did no such thing," added Millicent.

"I checked both of you out. Since you were involved almost from the beginning, I felt you would be as tenacious as pit bulls. I was counting on you to find the actual killers. As a private citizen, you can do things that I can't do. I don't know how you got your information or clues, but I would bet money that it wasn't legal. If I had gotten that same information, a talented lawyer would have gotten it thrown out. You don't have to play by the same rules. You got a confession. If I had gone into their home, chances are they wouldn't have confessed."

"Can I bill the department for my services?"

"Of course not. You're not certified, licensed private detectives. We never authorized or officially approved your work, so we owe you nothing but a profound 'Thank you.'"

"Maybe we'll get a license, so we can bill you next time," stated Darcy.

He laughed. "Don't you dare get a license, Mrs. Bower. Then you'll be bound by almost as many laws as I am." He winked and walked away.

"That A-hole manipulated us to solve this case for him!" Millie fumed.

"Yes, he did, but he's right. He didn't have access to the resources we had. So, I guess in a way, it works for both parties."

"What about the others, like Susan Baxter, who's making and selling counterfeit art? Or with the attorney's wife? That was murder too. And Satchel Hollis. He may be into human trafficking. They are all guilty of something."

"Yes, Millie. But there is more to Satchel than meets the eye. Yes, he deals in human trafficking. What he does is buy some people and send them to language and trade schools. He gives them jobs and additional training. Then he sponsors them to get green cards, and eventually citizenship. If he can, he helps the government shut down the real traffickers. He's an authentic hero, not a criminal."

"How did you find all that stuff out? We were together most of the time working on Sassy's case?" asked Millie, thoroughly impressed with Darcy.

"I asked Mickey to look into Satchel while we were tracking down Kevin's killer. Let's just enjoy this wonderful day for Sassy and Josh. We'll look at the others another day!"

They heard glass clinking. "May I have your attention, please? We have one announcement my mother wishes to make before we continue this celebration," called out Josh to the crowd of people.

Mrs. Turner got up and walked to the front and took the microphone from him. "Sassafras, would you come to the front, please?"

The room was silent as Sassy walked up front beside her new husband and mother-in-law.

Mrs. Turner gave her a big hug and spoke. "I'm so proud of my son, Joshua, for finding such a wonderful person to love and spend the rest of his life with." Sassy stood blushing at her mother-in-law's remarks. "Are you familiar with TOCO?"

"Yes, ma'am. That's the company that loaned the money to install the diesel pump at my store."

"That is an acronym, Turner Oil Company. My husband, Sterling, and I own that company."

"Okay, so you have the mortgage on my store?" Sassy asked.

"No, dear. Not anymore." She handed Sassy an envelope. "The document you signed a few weeks ago is in that envelope, and it's marked 'Paid-in-full.' It's yours now. Since you are family, you are part of the Turner Oil Company. That is your wedding present from Sterling and me. Welcome to the family!"

Sassy sheepishly turned to Josh and said, "You aren't really just a driver for the supply company that brings my stuff?"

"That's correct," he answered happily.

"So, you are rich?"

"I am rich now that I have you as my wife. And I also have a lot of money," he said as he leaned forward and kissed her. "We... are rich."

Once again, it was a wonderful day in the town of Bridgeton.

MURDER AT THE BLUE LIGHT CLUB

loria stepped out from behind the curtain to center stage in front of the band. She smiled at the crowd and looked around. From as close as the front row of tables, she was the spitting image of one of the brightest and most talented singers of the nineteen seventies. Gloria was wearing a flowing black low-cut dress and had a traditional pageboy hairstyle.

"Thank you for coming tonight as we celebrate the talented singer, Toni Tennille of the duo, The Captain and Tennille. I'd like to sing for you my personal favorite song, Lonely Nights, or as it's also known as, Angel Face."

The audience clapped as she glanced back and motioned for the band to start. As she waved her hand, and raised her head, the band played the lead in, and she belted the beginning of the song.

"Lonely nights, I cry myself to sleep.

"Tell me, what am I gonna do?

"Cause it's always you, to dry my tears…"

Suddenly her eyes grew wide, her mouth opened, and no words came out. A spot of red blossomed and spread on her chest. She dropped to the floor.

The band stopped playing immediately as the pianist stopped playing and ran to her, and kneeled down.

A woman in the audience screamed, and the rest of the audience sat stunned. The pianist called out, "Someone call nine-one-one! They shot her!"

James Bower jumped up from his seat at the table on the front row and ran to her. He took the cloth napkin from the table where he was sitting and placed it on her chest to stop the flow of blood.

As people realized what had happened, they began running for the exits. Daniel, James' father-in-law, pulled out his cell phone, and dialed the emergency number as he pushed his daughter, Darcy Jean, under the table.

A voice answered at the other end of the call. "What is your emergency?"

"I'm Daniel Christianson. I'm at The Blue Light Night Club. A woman has been shot. We need an ambulance and the police."

"Please stay on the line, sir. Are you in any direct danger?" she asked.

Daniel moved the phone away from his face and looked at it like it was a foreign object. "Someone is shooting, and one person's been hit. Get someone here….NOW!"

"Keep calm, sir. Emergency units are on the way. I hear screams in the background. Are there any others injured?"

Daniel looked around the room at the chaos and screaming people heading toward the exits. "I have no idea. What is the ETA for the units?"

"Hold on, sir. I'll check for you. Please keep calm, sir. I have an ETA of five minutes on the ambulance, and seven minutes on the police units, sir. Are there any more shots being fired? Any other injuries?" the voice asked.

"I don't know. I don't think so," answered Daniel. He looked up and saw James with a gun in his hand.

James was looking around for a shooter, then looked at Daniel, and shook his head, signaling the singer was dead.

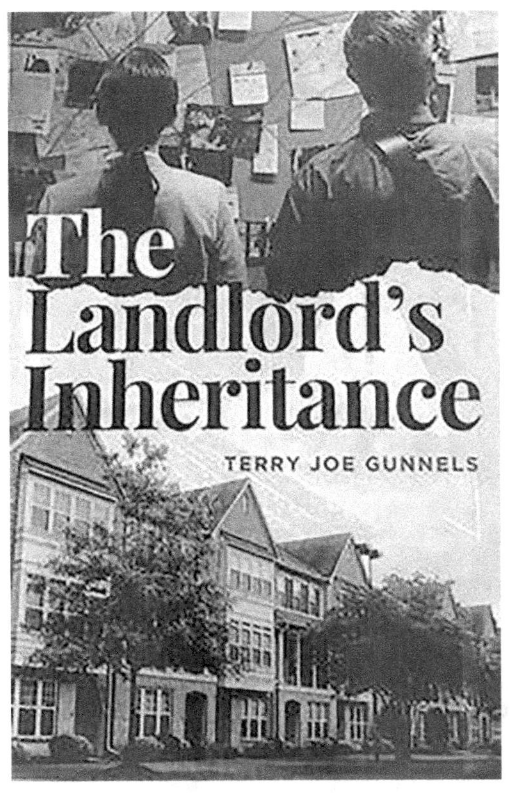

Siblings Mickey Ray and Darcy Jean are informed that the automobile disaster that caused the death of their Mother and their Father's multiple injuries including brain damage was not an accident but an attempted murder. The local police seem ambivalent, and their aunt comes in with a forgotten Power of Attorney signed by their Father, Daniel, and tries to take control of the Real Estate holdings. The brother and sister team begin a power struggle and are physically threatened by unknown thugs which results in Mickey's girlfriend's disappearance which she is presumed dead and Darcy Jean in hiding. James, Mickey's best friend, a disfigured Ex-Military Black Ops operative, assists in the hunt to put a stop to the "takeover."

Simple Detective Work, Internet Research, Adventure, Action and Suspense with a Sprinkle of Romance, and a Fast-Paced, Explosive ending are included in this book of intrigue.

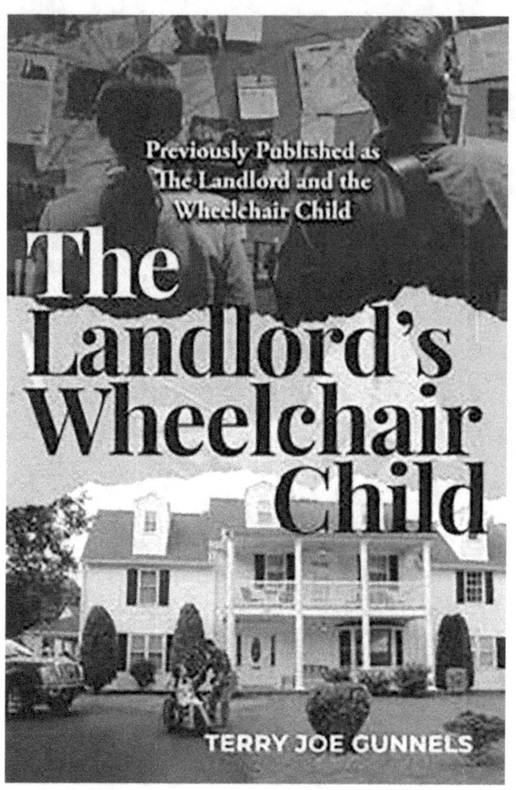

Landlord Mickey Ray Christianson is walking the grounds of his apartment complex late one afternoon, and he sees a little girl in a wheelchair sitting all alone. He sits down beside her and begins talking to her. He then finds out that her mother left her, intending to return. When the child's mother doesn't return, Mickey has the gut feeling that something has gone awry and calls his sister, Darcy, to run a background check on her parents. After Darcy gets permission from the Department of Child's Services to take custody of the child, Carrie, Mickey Ray, and his best friend, James, go hunting for Carrie's parents, assuming they were kidnapped. With help from some of James' past Black Ops teammates, a find-and-rescue operation takes place. After a suspenseful mission and a lot of action, Mickey reunites Carrie with her parents.

I hope you like Mickey and James' newest adventure as they dive headfirst into helping this little child. It is suspenseful to the very end.

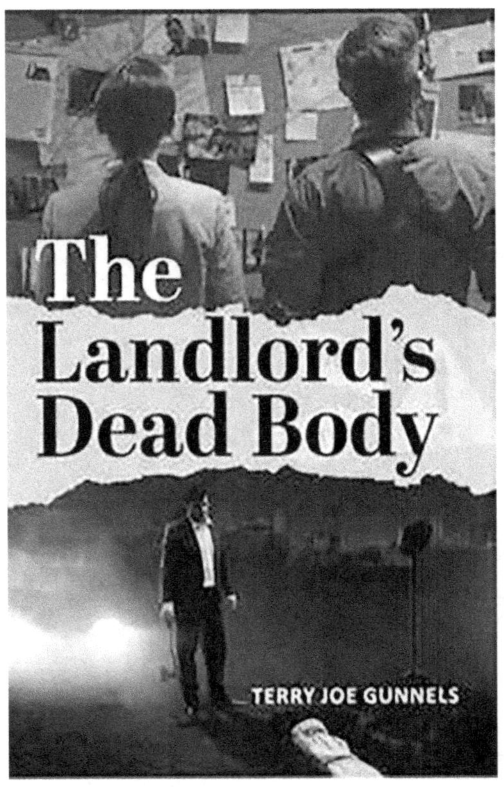

After many months of preparation, construction has begun on a new Apartment complex. On the very first day, a worker with a backhoe, digs up a body of a young lady. After the police identify the victim, it turns out that Mickey Ray Christianson and his sister Darcy Jean went to school with her. The victim, Betty Duncan was single, pregnant and lived with her mother in one of their apartments, so Mickey and his best friend and brother-in-law, James Bower set out to find her killer. They start with the obvious suspects, the baby daddy. Along the way, Mickey connects with one of his old schoolmates and thinks he is falling in love with her. After tracking down several leads and dead ends, the case is solved with a huge twist for Mickey and all involved.

I hope this one keeps you on the edge of your seat as it did me as I wrote it. Believe it or not, I didn't know "who dunnit" until the very end!

Mickey and James are back in action with this new action-thriller. The police answer Mickey's call to his ex-fiancée attending culinary school in Oregon. They tell him that Valerie is deceased, so Mickey flies out to pick up the body. The attractive police detective tells Mickey she has a "gut" feeling that it's murder. James, Mickey's best friend, gets a flight to help Mickey find the killer. James brings some others that helped them in earlier cases. Sexy Marie comes to do some undercover work, and little bombshell Alyssa comes to handle technical surveillance. The police detective and Mickey hit it off and she takes vacation time to join in the investigation. James obtains an armored Humvee, munitions, including rocket launchers he got on clearance from an anonymous arms dealer. They have run-ins with thugs, smugglers, and seriously evil men as they go to war to get justice for Mickey's ex-fiancée, Valerie. Ride along with the wild car chases, late-night raids, and the explosive fireball finish of this exciting new Landlord's adventure.

While driving from Oregon, Mickey Ray stops for lunch at a restaurant off the interstate. When someone approaches the table he's sharing with a beautiful young Asian lady, Mickey gets into an altercation, and is wounded in the fracas. He wakes up with total amnesia, in a hospital room with a gunshot wound in his side, being treated at an undisclosed Health Spa somewhere out west. During his recovery, Mickey learns the Spa caters to the rich and famous for their private retreats. And to top it off, the Yakuza (the Japanese Mafia) is trying to gain control of the Healing Health Spa. The Mongoose team is looking for Mickey and when they find him, agree to help save the spa from the takeover. The Mongoose team is soon aware a well-armed civilian army severely outnumbers them, and they are literally fighting for their lives. While there, the spa director assigns Mickey a personal assistant AI. As time progresses, the AI becomes sentient, or self-aware, and to add to the mix, thinks it has fallen in love with Mickey Ray.

Mickey Ray signs his family up for a ten-day Caribbean cruise in hopes of enjoying some much-needed rest and relaxation. However, just a few days into the voyage, chaos erupts when pirates descend onto the ship from a helicopter and seize control. Their demand: a ransom of one hundred million dollars from the CEO of one of the nation's largest banks in exchange for the safe return of his son- and daughter-in-law. In response, James calls in the Mongoose team, who covertly board the ship in the middle of the night and blend in among the passengers and crew. Soon after, James and Mickey are approached by Elisabeth, a CIA operative who had been placed undercover on board after the agency received intelligence about a possible pirate attack. When the pirates eventually escape with the hostages, the Mongoose team tracks them to uninhabited Caribbean islands and manages to rescue one of the captives-though the pirates slip through their grasp. With the help of Valerie A.I., the pirate leaders are later located in the ship's home port of Norfolk, Virginia. Determined to recover the ransom money-and hopefully the remaining hostage-James leads the team into one final operation. With the help of the undercover CIA operative, some quick thinking, and Valerie A.I.'s precision, the team brings the pirates to justice in a tense, action-packed finale with a surprise twist.

Mickey Ray is in his office one day and a beautiful young lady has an appointment to see him. Catherine Raynor of CRM Fashions has come to offer to sell him one of her apartment complexes. When Mickey asks why she wants to sell, she explains to him that there was a fire in her clothing factory. Because the fire was determined to be arson, insurance won't pay off. Even if she can prove that it was not arson the insurance payout will not cover enough to rebuild and save the family business. She needs cash, and the police are trying to pin the fire on her and send her to jail for insurance fraud. Mickey agrees to help her, so he calls in the Mongoose team to help prove her innocence.

A picture of the Author and one of his collectible autos.

The entire list of the author's works is available
at Amazon.com and Barnes & Noble.

And the author's website: terryjoegunnelsbooks.com

www.ingramcontent.com/pod-product-compliance
Lightning Source LLC
Chambersburg PA
CBHW071315150726
47997CB00002B/481